Cassie Clinton and the First Fatality

A Serenity Suites Cozy Mystery, Volume 1

Rachel Beattie

Published by Rachel Beattie, 2024.

This is a work of fiction. Similarities to real people, places, or events are entirely coincidental.

CASSIE CLINTON AND THE FIRST FATALITY

First edition. September 20, 2024.

Copyright © 2024 Rachel Beattie.

ISBN: 979-8227351258

Written by Rachel Beattie.

Chapter One

If there's one thing that's good about getting older - and believe me, what with creaking joints, ever-encroaching memory loss, and the feeling that the whole world is being run by children, there isn't much - it's not needing to use an alarm clock. I can guarantee to be awake long before sunrise no matter how late I stay up the night before. Except, of course, for the one morning when I really need to be up early.

I emerge from an unexpectedly deep sleep to see the sun streaming brightly through my window and realize with a lurch that my internal clock has finally decided to fail me.

Cassie Clinton, I berate myself. *You knew you'd live to regret that second glass of wine with dinner...* I fight off a yawn as I shuffle towards the bathroom and into the shower. I turn the thermostat up until it's hot enough to unknot the tension in my back and shoulders that always comes after lying too still for too long and think over my plans for the day. Even losing an hour or so this morning I should have just enough time to make it to my meeting. *But that certainly doesn't give me a license to luxuriate!* Reluctantly, I switch off the shower and reach for the thick cotton towel that is one of a few treats I've decided age and not-quite-yet-infirmity entitles me to.

It takes me a little longer than usual to get moving, but I'm soon dressed in a pretty floral blouse and the kind of slim-fit jeans many of my friends argue are too young to be worn by someone in their seventies. I like to think I can pull them off and take a moment to admire my reflection in the mirror on the wall. I finger-comb my grey bob into place and apply a coat of ruby-red lipstick, and just like that I'm ready to face the day.

My phone is already buzzing with notifications and I glance at it, thumbing through the most interesting and ignoring the rest while I check that my morning's meeting hasn't been canceled. Nope! Still on, and I check my watch to confirm I've still got just enough time to make it if I leave now. There's no time for breakfast, and no time to read my mail, either, though I snatch up the growing pile of letters from the mat and slip them into my purse as I pass.

I step out into the mid-morning chaos of Patterson, the small town I've lived in for the last ten years, and spot my neighbor standing wearily in her front yard. Tina Lombard is a doting mother of two tots with another on the way and she raises a cup of coffee in my direction as she keeps a canny eye on her son, who's happily chasing their cat around the yard. I wave to her and keep moving. Old Cooper Street is only a short distance from the rest of town. It's a bit dilapidated, truth be told, but I like to call its gently run-down style *rustic* and honestly, I wouldn't want to live anywhere else.

Downtown Patterson is hardly a roaring metropolis, which is just one of the reasons I love it. There's something charming about knowing everything about one another and feeling like you're part of a community, not just some face in the crowd. I pass two empty storefronts and a *for sale* sign and wish other people felt the same about this small town as I do. We don't get a lot of new arrivals which is a shame because Patterson has so much to offer. I grimace, as a car rattles noisily over a pothole and narrowly avoid tripping on an uneven paving stone. At least, we would have a lot to offer. All the town needs is a little bit of care and some financial investment.

It's all Ed's fault, I think to myself, before swiftly repenting of the thought. Edward Patterson was once the richest man in town - the town named after his grandfather, in case that needed spelling out. He had an interest in almost every business in town and was exactly the kind of man most people love to hate. Considering the way he treated my best friend - and his ex-wife - Mindy, it's not as if my dislike of him isn't justified. But he's been gone two months now and I'm of the generation that thinks it isn't right to speak ill of the dead.

I pause on the street corner and dig into my pocket for some change which I drop in the collection pot for a nearby homeless charity. Not thinking ill of the dead doesn't extend to forgetting everything they did while they were here on earth. Edward Patterson's sins could fill a book, and I think we're all better off without him.

"Morning, Cassie!"

I jump, narrowly avoiding a collision with Samuel Greenwood, who raises his reusable coffee cup in a salute.

"Are you on your way to Mindy's?" He waggles his eyebrows at me and pats the pocket of his checked shirt, making the half-dozen ballpoint pens it holds rattle together. "Ready to take me on at the Patterson Inquirer's daily crossword?"

I laugh and shake my head.

"Not this morning, Sam. I have a meeting to get to." I've fallen into a bad habit of wasting my mornings at Mindy's cafe, drinking endless refills of English breakfast tea and squabbling with the regulars. Anyone would think I was old!

"A meeting?" Sam purses his lips. "Fancy. No wonder you're all dressed up."

My smile stretches a little thin, and I pat Sam warmly on the shoulder.

"Another time," I promise, secretly vowing to avoid Mindy's next time I know Sam will be in residence. It's not that I don't like the guy, but I'm certainly not looking for a beau. Not now, not at my time in life, and certainly not Samuel Greenwood.

We say our goodbyes and I pick up the pace, not wanting to keep my friend waiting too much longer. It turns out I needn't have worried. The old Belgravia bowling alley is still pretty much a building site. When Louise Hamilton told me she planned to turn the Belgravia into a retirement community, I couldn't begin to imagine how that would work. I was just pleased to see anyone doing anything with the old building, which had been neglected for so long. I was a little sorry to see how much of the retro façade had been discarded, but I knew whatever Louise did she would give it her all and make it a roaring success.

I pick my way carefully through the double doors, dodging past workmen in hard hats, and trying to work out where, exactly, I might find my friend.

"Hey, lady! Watch it!"

I jump out of the way, narrowly avoiding being knocked over by two burly workmen manhandling a beam of wood in my direction, and brush against the side of the wall.

"Hey!" Another voice shouts, a little more kindly. "Take care, this paint is wet!"

"Oh!" I turn to look over my shoulder and sure enough, there is a smudge of deep purple staining my favorite blouse.

"Cassie!" Louise rounds the corner and spots me. "Oh no! Didn't anybody warn you about the paint?"

The workman gives an exaggerated cough and points towards a sign that I have completely failed to notice until this moment. *Wet paint.*

"It doesn't matter!" I say brightly, trying to convince myself that purple goes with green.

"Come on through to my office," Louise says, "We'll see if we can't wash that out before it sets." I open my mouth to tell her that it's going to take more than a rinse under a cold faucet to get a stain like this out of my favorite floral blouse, but my poor friend looks so frazzled that I don't want to add to her stress.

"It's fine," I insist, with a painfully bright smile. "I'm just sorry I didn't get here earlier." Someone, somewhere, fires up a power drill, and I have to shout to make myself heard over the noise. "What was it you wanted to see me about?"

Louise frowns at me and I repeat my question, but the power drill somehow finds an even more grating pitch, and in the end we give up. With a pantomime of sign language, Louise beckons me to follow her and we pick a cautious, careful route along crowded corridors, uneven flooring, and past dozens of workmen busily transforming the old, weatherbeaten bowling alley into something completely new and almost unrecognizable.

"In here!" Louise shouts over her shoulder, as she pushes open a red door that leads to a broom closet. *No,* I realize. *Not a broom closet, an office. A very small one.* I squeeze into the room behind her, and she closes the door, mercifully dropping the noise by a few precious decibels.

"That's better!" She gives me a quick hug, careful to avoid getting paint on herself, and then inches past me and around the desk that fills most of the available space in the room. She squeezes into her chair and points me towards one opposite her. It's piled high with papers and I hesitate for a moment, before gathering them together and placing them carefully on the desk between us so I can sit down.

"You wanted to see me?" I say, tucking my hair behind my ears, and smiling. "This place looks amazing, by the way!"

"It's a building site." Louise smiles, tiredly. "But it'll look great when it's done."

"I don't doubt it!" I look around the small office and can see, even amongst the chaos, touches of my young friend's personality. She might be exhausted, and this job might be a huge one, but Louise Hamilton is in her element. I'm pleased. She has had more than her fair share of knocks, but after almost a decade slaving away as Ed Patterson's Personal Assistant she is finally embarking on a project that's all her own. And it looks as if spending so many years so close to the businessman from hell might have benefitted her. She certainly seems to have learned a few things about project management.

An awkward silence has fallen between us and I realize Louise is waiting for the perfect introduction to whatever it is she wants to say. I decide to put her out of her misery and lean forward with a smile I hope is encouraging.

"Well, come on then. You don't have time to sit around and stare at me all day. What's this meeting all about?"

It's as if my questions open the floodgates, and Louise speaks so fast her words rush out, tripping over each other in their eagerness to be heard.

"Well, you see, it's like this… The project is going well. There's been a few funding hiccups here and there but I'm sure I'll be able to iron them out easily enough. We have a bunch of interested tenants and our first resident is already in the building. Joe. You'll like him. He's a character. And the other people that plan to move in are all wonderful. As are the staff, only…" She stops for breath. "We need a manager."

"What do you mean?" I laughed. "You're an excellent manager!"

"Project managing, yes." Louise nods. "But this role… It's more… Residential."

I stare at her nonplussed for a moment, trying to make sense of her words. At last, the pieces of the jigsaw slot into place.

"Louise… Are you offering me a job?" I pause and tug at the sleeve of my blouse. "Or trying to sell me a room?"

"Neither!" Louise beams at me, her smile bordering on desperate. "Both. I'm looking to hire a lifestyle manager to run things on-site here once we get our first cohort of residents moved in. It's a great job, and I need a great person to take it on."

"I'm sure you do, but that isn't me!" I laugh, but the sound is a little unconvincing to my own ears. "And I have a perfectly good house already."

"Then you wouldn't need to live on site. It's optional." Louise is getting a little desperate, and I begin to wonder just how many people she's had this conversation with so far today.

"Lifestyle manager. Isn't that the sort of role you should have filled before the place began to take in residents?" There's a steely note to my voice that I don't even try to hide.

"You're right! You're right. We should. We did! Only... They pulled out at the last moment. Now everything is running a little bit behind schedule and if we don't get a manager in place it will delay things even more. The whole project could fall apart." She tugs worriedly on an ornamental S-shaped pendant she wears around her neck. "What if it wasn't a permanent position? What if you just took it on for six months? The pay is good, and it is the perfect job for you."

There's a knock at the door that keeps me from replying and Louise lets out a desperate little squeak.

"Yes?"

The door swings open, and an old man with a craggy, weather-beaten face leans into the room.

"Lou, honey, you have to help me. These workmen have me practically barricaded in my room, and -" He spots me and straightens before giving us the kind of smile that can only be called rakish. "I'm very sorry, I didn't realize you had company."

"Joe, this is my friend Cassie. Joe Price is our very first resident who I was just telling you about. He's very understanding about the amount of upheaval he's moved right into the middle of. Let me come and see what I can do to help..." Louise jumps to her feet and edges round the desk, laying a conciliatory hand on my shoulder as she passes me. "I'll be back in a moment, Cassie," she says. "Please think about it, at least!"

I nod and stay right where I am as she hurries off to resolve yet another problem.

A job offer? I certainly wasn't expecting that to happen to me today. Not that I'm not interested. Since Louise first told me about the Serenity Suites project, I thought it sounded like a wonderful idea. *For maybe ten or twenty years in the future.* I toss my head. I may not be as young as I used to be, but I'm certainly not residential home ready yet! I set my jaw, determined to refuse Louise as politely as I can when she comes back. Maybe I can help her come up with another option. Between us, we have quite a social network. I'm sure there must be someone in the Venn diagram of people we know who would be perfect for the role.

Louise has been gone a lot more than a minute, and after a while I reach for my purse, pull out my phone, and plan to work a few rounds of a word game I am more than a little bit addicted to. The tips of my fingers brush the pile of envelopes I scooped up on my way out of the door this morning, and I choose to read my mail instead of my phone. I come to regret that decision pretty much immediately. Shuffling the envelopes in order of size, I open the top one and smooth out the letter inside, my mouth falling open in horrified shock as I read it through once, twice, three times, trying to make sense of the printed words in front of me.

Dear Ms. Clifton, it begins. My eyes narrow, and I skim over the pleasantries to reach the real details of the letter. The words swim and I lean in closer to make sure I'm reading them right.

I'm being evicted?

Chapter Two

"Evicted? What do you mean?"

I reach into my purse and pull out the letter, thrusting it in Mindy's direction.

After reading it, I couldn't wait around for Louise to come back. I scribbled a note explaining my disappearance and hightailed it out of the building. Panic kept me walking all the way to Min's, and even now, with a cup of sweetened black tea and my best friend on hand, I'm not feeling much better.

"They can't do this, can they?" Mindy asks as she reads over the letter before passing it back to me. "They have to give notice. Who is your landlord?"

I look at her, and the sharpness of my gaze is enough to make her realize my landlord is no longer with us. Edward Patterson owned half the town, and now that he's gone, that property has passed onto...whoever he bequeathed it to.

"Ah." She pauses. And when she speaks again, her voice is ringing with false cheer. "Well, the notice, then. Whoever they are, they can't just evict you without any warning."

I smooth out the letter and trace a few words with one fingertip, reading aloud.

"Further to our previous letters..." I wince. "I need to get a bit better at opening my mail."

It's not like that, really. I just have a knack for knowing at a glance whether an envelope is going to be worth opening or not. Correspondence from friends, which is a rarity in the Internet age, I always open immediately. Then there are birthday cards, Christmas cards, postcards, and anything that looks like a coupon that might save me money. Bills and official notices are far less interesting. I shift uncomfortably in my seat. There's more than one bill I've been actively avoiding lately, and I probably need to start dealing with them as well, unless I want to end up destitute as well as homeless.

"So what are you going to do?"

"There's not a lot I can do." I take a sip of my drink, relishing the sweetness. "If Ed were still here, I might have tried to reason with him."

Mindy's eyes flash with irritation.

"I know he was a terrible husband, and a terrible human a lot of the time, but I won more than one argument with that man, and I would try my hardest to win this one." I sigh. "But now he's gone."

"Do you even know who inherited his property portfolio?" Mendy laughed, bitterly. "I can tell you none of it came my way! I expect the bulk of it went to that woman."

Our eyes meet. Jessica Patterson, Ed's second wife, his present window, made no secret of the abundant life she lived while married to the richest man in town. Oddly enough, since her husband's death two months ago, she hasn't been seen swanning around Patterson quite so much. And her money has stayed happily in the bank, accruing interest instead of being splashed around town with abandon.

"Well that isn't going to help me," I remark with a glum smile. "I don't think I've spoken more than five words to her in the last five years!"

"You aren't missing much." Mindy rolls her eyes. She has always had a very dismissive opinion of her replacement and she doesn't care who knows it.

I look over the letter once more, even though its contents are pretty much committed to memory by now. The legalese gives me two weeks to get my things together and vacate the place that's been my home, my pride and joy, for the last ten years. Two weeks! Even if I walked into a new rental today, that wouldn't be enough time to make arrangements. And then there's the fact that I don't exactly have an income at the moment. I glance around Mindy's bustling coffee shop, momentarily envious that my friend has her own business with a cute little apartment upstairs and I have nothing. *Not nothing.* I snatch up my letter, determined not to just accept my fate without a fight.

"Well, maybe she'll listen to reason. Losing her husband like that might have given her a dose of empathy." I swallow the last of my tea and stand up, drawing a big breath in and squaring my shoulders. "There's only one way to find out."

• • • •

THE PATTERSON SKYLINE is dotted with shabby-ish cottages, run-down community buildings, and slightly neglected green space. But there's one building that dominates. Edward Patterson's grand house is one of the oldest buildings in town, with all the old features and new additions that make it striking and unique. It's known locally as *the mansion,* and honestly, if ever a building deserved such a name, it's this one. In a town where nothing is quite as neat and cared for as it ought to be, the mansion shines. I've always loved it, and when Mindy lived here, was a frequent visitor. Even now, two months after the death of its owner, the mansion still stands out. Its manicured lawns and elegant façades are kept spotless by a team of staff, and I see several people busily working away as I stride up the driveway, my eviction notice clasped tightly in my hand. The front door is open, so I don't have to knock, and I slip in, surprised that chaos seems to be the theme of the day. I can't help but compare the Serenity Suites building site with the crowd of staff bustling around the inside of the mansion, and I'm about to stop someone and ask what's going on when a shriek halts me in my tracks.

"What are you doing?" The shrill voice demands. "That can't stay there! Tonight is supposed to be a party! The last thing we'll want is some dreary old statue staring down at us in judgment!"

Jessica. I remember that this is the woman I've come all this way to talk to and draw a breath, skirting around the staff who are meekly cleaning and reorganizing and arranging things to suit their capricious boss.

"Jessica! Good morning, dear!"

A pair of low-lidded, gray eyes fix on me.

"It's Cassie," I lay a light hand on my chest, making an introduction that ought to be unnecessary. We've met before. "Cassie Clifton."

"I know who you are," Jessica looks bored. I suppose it's a change from infuriated. "What are you doing here? Can't you see I'm busy?"

"Then I'll only take up a minute of your time." I hold up the letter, praying that Jessica can't see my hand shake. "I need to speak to you about this."

"If it's a complaint, then I don't have time to hear it!" Jessica says. "I can direct you to my lawyer, or... No! Not there!"

I turn my head and see a stone statue that looks like it ought to be in a museum, not a person's home. Three people are trying to move it, and I can tell from the strain on their faces that is not an easy task.

"It's about my house," I say, deciding I'd better just be upfront. "I had an eviction notice this morning, quite out of the blue. I'm sure it's just a simple mistake,"

"I can't help you!" Jessica shakes her head. "If you have a query about business or money or property, it's nothing to do with me!"

I sigh, feeling very deflated, but when I glance her way, I see a shadow flicker across Jessica's face that I don't think has anything to do with me.

"Very well, then. Who's your business manager? Or your lawyer? Is there somebody I can speak to about this? What should I do?"

Jessica lets out an exaggerated sigh and turns towards me, folding her toned arms and glaring at me.

"I told you. It's nothing to do with me! I have no say over anything at all. I'm only the widow!"

I'm confused. I open my mouth to ask what on earth she's talking about, but a door slams somewhere in the building, and we both turn toward the sound. Heavy footsteps strike the parquet floor, echoing over the low rumble of chaos, and I see a tall, dark-haired figure striding confidently down the stairs.

"Excuse me," Jessica shoves past me, eager to intercept the stranger on his way to the door. I hesitate for all of a minute before following her. Whoever this man is, he has Jessica's attention, and that has my attention. Maybe this is some kind of business manager who can help me out of my current predicament.

"You can't be here! I told you that already." Jessica takes a breath but her quarry has barely slowed his pace. She plants herself right in his path, wobbling in heels that are far too high to be comfortable. "Well?" Her voice rings with challenge, and it's enough to make the man stop and look at her. He is pretty handsome. A good twenty years too young for me, but certainly easy on the eyes. Or he would be if he wasn't scowling.

"Well?" There's something vaguely mocking in his voice and his expression as he parrots her word back to her, but I don't think that Jessica notices. She stamps her foot.

"Are you finished? In case you haven't noticed, I'm trying to get ready for a party. Is there anything else you need, or can I access my own rooms in my own house at last?"

"It isn't your house, Jessica," the man says, with a smile. "Staying here is a courtesy until you can get something else figured out. Which is fine. Throw as many parties as you want. But do be aware that I have compiled a detailed inventory of all the pieces that belong here. If anything was to go missing..."

"Excuse me?" Jessica's voice is so shrill it makes me wince. "Are you accusing me of theft?"

"Not accusing." Is it my imagination or is this stranger now fighting an urge to laugh? "Just reminding you of your responsibilities while you remain here."

"What about you?" Jessica asks, although I can tell she doesn't want to know the answer. "Are you staying in town? In case I need to reach you."

"I'll be around." The man says, glancing at a very expensive watch. "I have a meeting to get to right now, but the rest of my day is free." He smiles, and again I get the feeling he's mocking Jessica, although she doesn't seem to notice. "Of course I wouldn't miss your party. I assume I'm invited?"

There's a long, awkward pause before Jessica answers in a voice that is too high and too loud to be entirely genuine.

"Of course!" She seems to remember all at once I'm standing there. She turns to me, all sweetness in contrast to the greeting I received a few moments earlier. "Cassie will be there as well, won't you Cassie? Everybody will. Half the town is invited!"

"Great." The stranger says, giving me a brief nod. "Then I wouldn't miss it. But now I have to go." He turns on his heel and stalks out of the building, leaving Jessica and me to stare after him. I'm desperate to know what that was all about, and who this man is. I don't recognize him, but there is something vaguely familiar about his attitude. I take a breath, realizing this is probably the last chance I'm going to have to speak to Jessica before she gets subsumed by party preparations again.

"So, about this eviction notice..."

"You heard the man," Jessica says, with a toss of her blonde curls. "Everyone will be at the party tonight. I'm sure you'll be able to sort it out then. Now, if you'll excuse me, I have a lot of things to get ready." She claps her hands and out of nowhere, a short, squat woman with straw-colored hair appears at Jessica's side, ready to take instructions with an eager, submissive little curtsey. "Cassie is just leaving. Show her out, won't you? Then we can go make a start on the linens..."

Chapter Three

I decide not to go back to Mindy's once Jessica makes it clear I'm no longer welcome at the mansion. I already know my best friend's opinion of her so-called replacement, and I am in no mood to listen to Min's list of all the reasons why her ex-husband's now-widow is the worst thing to ever happen to him, to Mindy, and to all of us in Patterson. I can't say I disagree with Mendy on a lot of her complaints, but staying stuck in bitterness over the past isn't going to help anyone. It certainly isn't going to help me. My problems are a lot more pressing, and I decide that I need to make an action plan. And that means I need to know exactly where I stand right now. *You can't make a map if you don't know where you're starting from.* I make my way towards the bank, thinking that the first and most important thing I need to do is figure out the lie of the financial land. I know I can manage all of this through the internet. My niece, Merry, and every other friend I have under the age of forty are permanently trying to encourage me to digitize even more my life. I know there's an app for this, but I'm not quite ready to sign everything over to my evil robot overlords quite yet. Besides, running my life through a computer screen would keep me from spending time out and about in Patterson proper, seeing my friends and my neighbors face-to-face.

The Patterson branch of the Stellar National Bank is a small one, and I know each of the three-person-staff by name. Travis Lee, the manager, is barricaded away in his office with a client. I can just see his prematurely balding head bobbing around as he gets energized, explaining the latest and greatest investment opportunities to his current victim. I keep moving. Both of the customer service desks are clear, and I see the two tellers, Tracey and Jane, eye each other competitively as they see me approach.

"Morning, girls!" I say, wondering which of them is going to be the first to claim my custom.

"Afternoon!" Tracey pipes up, checking her watch. "It's 12:05."

"Is it?" Jane jumps up from behind her desk. "I'd better take my lunch break! Do you think you can handle this?"

"We'll be just fine," I tell her. "You go and enjoy your break." I wave as she totters off, leaving me at the mercy of her friend.

"How can I help you today, Ms. Clinton?" Tracey asks, tapping a few keys on her computer as I line my bank cards up in front of her.

"Cassie," I remind her. "I just need to check a few account balances."

"Of course." She glances at my first card, taps in the number, and beams at me as the computer whirs into life. "You do realize you can do all this at home on the Internet?"

"I do, thank you." I smile. "But if I did that I wouldn't be able to come and talk to you now, would I? That's a very pretty ring you're wearing." She glances down at her hands, wiggling her fingers to demonstrate an elegant manicure to match the elegant engagement ring she is now sporting. "Did that nice young Christopher finally pop the question?"

"He did!" She beams. "We're going to get married in the spring!"

"How wonderful! I suppose you'll be saving for the wedding, then?"

"Yes." Tracey groans. "Don't remind me. Everything is so expensive. The wedding, the honeymoon. I want to find a new place to live together." She pulls a face. "Don't get me wrong, I love living with my sister, and Chris has a perfectly nice apartment, but..."

"You want somewhere that's both of yours," I say with a nod. "I understand that!"

She nods and prints off the first of my statements.

"You didn't hear it from me," she says. "But I've got my eye on one of the new developments. I heard from Tasha, who heard it from Ellen, who heard it from Peter, who said that the town committee is discussing the creation of several new houses on Old Cooper Street."

"What's that?" I tilt my head, my heart jackhammering in my chest. Old Cooper Street is *my* street. I know every building on the block, and there certainly isn't space for anything new.

"Oh yes," Tracey continues, pulling up my second account and printing the statement. "They're bulldozing those poky little houses that are already there. It's about time they built something nice."

"What about the people that live there?" My throat constricts. "In those poky little houses?"

Tracey blinks at me.

"Well, they'll have to move, won't they? The person who inherited Mr. Patterson's business affairs is excited about developing the area." She beams at me. "He's in the office discussing a few options right now with Mr. Lee."

I turn my head, squinting through the frosted glass windows of the branch manager's office, wishing I could see through them. This is the man who is responsible for my eviction, then. This is the man I need to appeal to for a reprieve. My heart sinks. And it sounds like he's already three steps ahead of me.

"Is there anything else I can do for you today, Ms. Clifton?" Tracey asks with another syrupy smile. "Let me guess, another cruise?"

"No," I say, snatching my printed statements a little more sharply than I mean to. "I need to make some changes and start saving." I smile stiffly. "It sounds like both of us are going to be on a budget for a while."

I say my goodbyes and turn to leave the bank, hesitating as I reach the doorway. I wonder if there's any way I could at least get a look at the man who is currently planning to redevelop my house without me in it. I want some idea of what he looks like. Maybe I already know him! I know just about everybody in Patterson, and if this is someone Ed Patterson valued enough to bequeath him his property portfolio...

"Are you alright there, Cassie?" Tracey calls, seeing my hesitation.

"Oh, fine!" I wave my bank statements at her and start moving again, regretting that this is yet another missed opportunity to make progress in the area I really need to make progress in. I'm not watching where I'm going, so it should come as no surprise when I collide bodily with a man making his way into the bank as I'm trying to leave it.

"Oof!"

"Ouch!"

I look up into the sort of handsome face that usually adorns men's aftershave commercials. It's certainly not the type of face you usually see strolling around Patterson at lunchtime on a Tuesday.

"I'm sorry, ma'am," he says, taking a hasty step back before laying a light hand on my shoulder. "Did I hurt you?" He has the sort of smooth southern drawl that makes my knees weak.

"No!" I giggle, and smile, and then remind myself I am old enough to be this heartthrob's mother. *Or even his grandmother!* My smile dims a little.

"Are you sure?" He winks. "You look a little dazed."

"No!" I shake my head, and the room starts to spin. I swallow. "No, I'm fine." I hurry past him and out into the street, then can't resist turning to get another look. What is it about all the handsome strangers coming to Patterson today? And why are they all far too young for me?

• • • •

"SO WHAT ARE YOU GOING to do?"

If there's one person a girl can always go to for advice, it's her hairdresser, and mine is no exception. Silvio runs his hands through my silky silver hair and peers at my reflection in the mirror.

"About what?" I ask, petulantly flipping a page in the fashion magazine in my lap. We're almost at the end of my appointment - an emergency fit-in when I realized I have a party to go to tonight, and I desperately need a little pampering. Silvio has patiently listened to a chaotic rundown of my day thus far, as well as sympathetically clucking as I told him my woes about the looming eviction.

"About what?" He rolls his eyes. "About your living situation. Honestly, Cass, you can't expect it all to just go away while you keep your head in the sand." He fluffs my hair. "Especially not when your head looks this good, even if I do say so myself."

"Thank you." I give my reflection an appraising look and can't help but smile. He may not have done much, barely a trim and a tidy-up, but there's no telling the difference a decent blow-dry from a good stylist can make. "I look ten years younger!"

"Then you're all ready for the party tonight. Have you decided yet what you're going to wear?"

I sigh and glance down at the fashion spread in my magazine. Every model on the page looks amazing and my wardrobe is starting to feel a fair bit tired. *Tough*, I tell myself. *You can just learn to make do. There must be something in there that will work for a party at the mansion.* I think of my last update to my holiday wardrobe and wonder if I can repurpose any of my cruise dresses for this evening and slowly my mood brightens. Silvio catches sight of the change in my countenance and gives me an impromptu hug.

"That's more like it. Remember what we always say, darling. You're never fully dressed without a smile!" He mugs in the mirror for me and I pat him on the cheek, wondering if I can smuggle him along to the party as my plus-one. Considering I only barely scored an invite myself, I doubt it, but I'm grateful for his support this afternoon.

"And don't worry about the house," he tells me, waving away my efforts to pay him for his time. "You save your money until you're settled into your new place. What about that new retirement community?"

"Silvio." I snap my purse closed and toss my head, making my new choppy hair bounce. "It's a retirement community. For old people."

He says nothing and my eyes narrow.

"*Older than me* people."

"Fine." He holds his hands up in surrender. "Forget I said anything. Only...it just seemed like it might be the perfect fit. They're looking for tenants. You're looking for somewhere to live. And I've seen some of these places. They are *fancy*. More hotel than care home." He lowers his voice. "And probably stuffed to the gills with eligible bachelors..."

"Ha!" I bark, brushing off his words. "That shows what you know. There's one man who moved in already and he might be a bachelor but he certainly isn't eligible. He's..." I frown, noticing the smirk on my stylist's face and realizing that I've already said too much. "Never mind. I'm sure Serenity Suites is a great option but not for me." I shake my head. "Not for me. Now, I'd better get a wriggle on. Lots to do to get ready for the party!"

"Remember darling, I want to hear all about it tomorrow! Are you free in the morning? We should do brunch."

I wave and hurry out of the salon, thinking over the rest of my errands to get done today. My phone rings noisily in my bag and I stop in the street, digging around to try and liberate it. *Louise.* Guilt makes my stomach flip. I just walked out of our meeting earlier, and as I slide my thumb across the screen I register this isn't the first time today she's tried to call me. With haste, I click to accept her call and press my phone to my ear.

"Louise?"

"Cassie! Good, you're still alive."

"Of course I'm still alive." My voice is crotchety and I don't even try to hide it. What is it with everyone acting like I'm about to drop off my perch at any moment?

"I just mean that I'm glad you're ok," Louise says, brightly. "When I couldn't get hold of you...and you disappeared so quickly earlier...I just wanted to make sure everything was alright." She pauses. "You are alright, aren't you?"

"Yes." I turn the irritation down a notch, deciding that my friend didn't mean anything, and if I'm feeling sensitive about my age that's hardly her fault.

"So, did you have any more time to think about it?"

"About what, dear?" I stroll along the street, pausing to admire a window display in one of the stores. I'm not really listening as Louise makes her job and accommodation pitch one more time. My attention is caught by something happening inside the store. A tall dark-haired man is lining up purchases like they're going out of style. I squint, making out a dusty old portrait, a carved wooden elephant, and some kind of vase that looks older than dirt. These purchases aren't going out of style, they were never in style to begin with. Something about the man's posture strikes me as familiar, and as he turns his head I suck in a gasp. I've seen him before. He is the first, and possibly only, person I've ever seen capable of rendering Jessica Patterson speechless, and in her own house, too. *And that certainly makes him worthy of a little investigation.*

"Louise, I'm sorry dear. I'll have to call you back."

Chapter Four

My curiosity gets the better of me and after debating with myself for a minute, I slip into Annabelle's antiques store. I'm not planning to buy anything. I'm hardly even looking at anything. My attention is fixed solely on the small drama unfolding by the cash register.

"I don't understand, sir," Annabelle Cricket sounds almost tearful as she tries to reason with the furious man in front of her. "The price is quite clearly marked on these items. If you'd like to purchase them, or if you want us to hold them for you..."

"No, I don't want to purchase them!" The man hisses. "I want to know where you got them from. They shouldn't be for sale at all!"

"Sir?" Annabelle's voice shakes.

"Where did you get these from? Who donated them? I have a right to know who is stealing -"

"Stealing? What seems to be the problem here?"

Uh oh. Both Annabelle and the stranger turn at the sound of a confident voice, as Patterson's popular sheriff, Bob Cooper steps into the fray. He's wearing his usual non-uniform uniform of jeans and a checked shirt, with his sheriff's badge pinned neatly to his lapel. He smiles, but it's not the kind of smile you return.

"Afternoon, Annabelle." He greets the tearful shop owner before turning to survey her customer. "It looks like you're having something of a disagreement. Maybe I can help."

"Are you the sheriff?" The stranger asks, not looking the least bit deterred by the involvement of law enforcement.

"Certainly am." Bob places his hands on his hips, his smile transforming into something more serious. "Care to tell me what's going on here?"

"That's what I'd like to know!" The man holds up a portrait of an attractive, if stern, looking woman dressed in the fashions of a hundred years previously. I subtly squint at the name-plate and read *Aunt Simone*. The stranger turns and points out a collection of other knickknacks and trinkets lined up on the register. "I want to know where these came from. They shouldn't be here. They shouldn't be for sale."

"And why is that?"

"They belong to me. They've been in my family for a long time. That's why I'd like to learn how they wound up here, on sale for a fraction of what they should be worth. I know I didn't donate them, so who did?"

"Annabelle?" Bob turns to look at her, a frown settling uncomfortably on his face. "You keep a record of who donates things, don't you?"

"Not these." Annabelle shakes her head, looking even more like she's about to burst into tears. "They were with a collection of other items left on the doorstep when I came into work the other day. People quite often leave bags and boxes of donations if they can't get in to donate when we open. And I haven't been in for a day or two." She sniffs. "Things were piling up."

"That's convenient."

"Hey!" Bob's head swivels from Annabelle to the stranger.

"I'm just saying it's convenient." He shrugs his broad shoulders. "Precious family heirlooms are stolen and turn up here for sale, and this lady's got no idea how they got here."

"*This lady* is a pillar of the Patterson community." Bob folds his arms and stares down the stranger. "If it comes down to taking her word over yours, I'd think twice before casting aspersions on her character."

The stranger smiles, a sad, self-deprecating sort of smile, and he nods, slowly.

"I see. Patterson protects its own."

"Patterson doesn't entertain nonsense accusations. If you'd like to come down to the station, I'd be more than happy to take your statement and we can do some investigating. If you think these items were stolen, then I'll need to know where they were stolen from. And when."

"Never mind." The stranger shakes his head. "Forget it. Perhaps I was mistaken." He thrusts the portrait into Bob's arms and storms out of the shop, banging the door behind him. I watch him go through the window, wondering, for the second time that day, just who this stranger is, and what has brought him to Patterson.

"I didn't know these weren't regular donations, I swear! If these items are stolen then of course I won't sell them. I just can't believe that I had stolen goods in my possession! That I might have been - committing a crime!" Annabelle sobs through an explanation, and Bob awkwardly pats her on the shoulder with his free hand, while he stands the portrait carefully on the ground. He is out of his element with a crying lady, and he looks around for assistance, his gaze landing on mine with relief.

"Cassandra! Excellent! Come and reassure Ms. Cricket she did nothing wrong, won't you?"

I hurry forward and put an arm around Annabelle's shaking shoulders. Her sobs subside, and she looks at me through red, watery eyes.

"I don't even know what he was talking about," she says, her voice wobbling. "He said these are family heirlooms. What family?"

"Have you ever seen him before?" Bob asks. I can tell from the tone of his voice and the tilt of his head that his small-town-sheriff Spidey senses are engaged.

"He was at the mansion earlier." My lips turn down in a grimace. "Having a fairly prickly conversation with Jessica Patterson. She certainly seemed to know exactly who he was and what he was doing here, so perhaps she might be able to help. It doesn't look like his mood has improved any. What a bad-tempered individual. I hate to say it, but I think I'm on Jessica's side with this one." I pat Annabelle on the arm. "And yours, of course."

Bob nods, but I can tell from the twitch in his jaw that the very last thing he wants to do is hike over to the mansion and have a heart-to-heart with Jessica Patterson.

"She's having a party tonight," I say. "Maybe Mr. Sunny Disposition will be invited." I smile. "I can see what I can find out if you like?"

Bob rolls his eyes. He knows I have a habit of sticking my nose in where is not wanted. Or as I like to call it, *being neighbourly*.

"How about we just write this off as an unfortunate misunderstanding?" He glances warily at Annabelle, who noisily blows her nose into a vintage, lace-trimmed handkerchief. "Would you like me to follow things up at the station?"

"No." Annabelle shakes her head, then scoops up the selection of items that had agitated her customer. "But I certainly will be a bit more careful about what I sell. Stolen heirlooms indeed! What sort of business does he think I run?"

· · · ·

REASSURING ANNABELLE that nobody could ever consider her the criminal mastermind behind a ring of thieves operating in downtown Patterson takes a lot longer than I expect, but it does yield some good personal results too. With my finances what they are I could do with making a quick buck or two of my own, and I manage to turn our conversation towards the sorts of prices she pays and the kinds of items she's actively looking for.

"I can certainly help you out with a few things," I say, injecting my voice with a brightness I don't entirely feel. "Maybe I could drop a box or two in this week?"

"That would be lovely, Cassie. Though only things you want to get rid of." She eyes me and a glimmer of her old sparkle starts to show again. "And only things that are yours to begin with!"

I laugh.

"Hand on heart, Annabelle, it'll be my very own junk that I'm very much in need of parting with." *And profiting from*. I don't say this last part out loud, but somehow she seems to sense it. She looks at me seriously.

"Is everything alright, Cassie? You don't quite seem your usual spirited self today." She sniffs again and reaches for her handkerchief. "I know my excuse - thief, indeed! But are you quite well?"

"Quite well!" I nod and force my lips to stretch in a smile I think is almost convincing. "Just trying to deal with too many problems at once, as usual." I think guiltily of Louise and wonder if I ought to call her back now, but then I see time is rapidly ticking on and I still have a party to get ready for. I take one last look around the store and come to rest on Annabelle wanting to reassure myself she is going to be fine before I leave her alone, and my gaze catches on a piece of dusty furniture in one dark, overlooked corner of the store. I'm walking towards it almost before I'm aware of it. "Where did this come from?"

"Oh, that was waiting outside as well." Annabelle frowns. "The same day as the other donations...wait, you don't think that's stolen too?" Her voice takes on a warning quiver and I'm quick to shake my head and settle her with a smile. I'm not being entirely honest, though, because I've seen a small end-table like this before, only I can't quite remember where. It's that dark, lacquered wood that looks dated now but was quite fashionable back in the day, and when I slide open the drawer I see there's a couple of scraps of paper inside. Old letters, perhaps, forgotten by the donor. A curious impulse makes me pull them out all the same, and I catch sight of a familiar name. *Edward Patterson.*

"Cassie?"

I shove the papers into my purse and turn to smile at Annabelle.

"I think I'd like you to put this aside, Annabelle, if you don't mind. Oh, don't worry, I'm sure it's not stolen!" I lie through my teeth. "But I certainly don't want you to sell it to somebody else before I have a chance to come back and take another look at it. What do you say? Will you hide it for me?"

Annabelle offers me a conspiratorial grin, and together we manage to maneuver the small - but surprisingly heavy - end table out of sight into her back room. I really do take my leave, then, and am halfway home before I recall the papers I shoved out of sight. I ease them free and read over them again, squinting to decipher the handwritten words.

I'm not asking for anything from you...this was my mistake as much as yours...my child doesn't need to know who their father is and neither does anybody else...

My eyebrows lift and I glance around, fearful of somehow betraying the hint of scandal I'm now holding my very own hands. I read back over the snippet, but it's almost like trying to untangle a code without any kind of key to unlock it. *Edward Patterson fathered a child that nobody knows about?* That's the sort of news that could blow up a small town like Patterson. *Not to mention hurting a whole lot of people.* I think of Jessica, and then again of Mindy, before folding the letters away and stowing them carefully in my purse for safekeeping. *Well, we've gone this long without knowing a word about it. I don't suppose there's any reason to break the news now.*

I pick up my pace, hurrying home where I'll be able to hide this secret safely away from prying eyes, and begin to wonder just who is responsible for the other items, along with the suspicious end-table, winding up in Annabelle's antique store, instead of staying safely in the mansion where they belong.

Chapter Five

I'm just putting the finishing touches to my make-up when there's a knock at my front door. Taking one last look at my reflection in the mirror, I smile, fix a stray strand or two of hair, and grab my purse before hurrying to answer it.

"Cassie?" The knock comes again, and I open the door, smiling to see Louise standing there in front of me looking not unlike a fairytale princess. Her blue dress sparkles with sequins and I feel a little under-dressed, despite being rather fond of my old-faithful little black dress.

"Louise!" I beam at her. "You look lovely!"

"So do you!" She laughs and we very carefully hug one another. I step back, welcoming her into my house, but she shakes her head, glancing down towards the road.

"I can't stop. I'm on my way to -"

"To the mansion?" I ask. "So am I! And I know exactly why you're here now. I never called you back, did I? I'm sorry." I think about telling her story of the odd encounter I had in Annabelle's store this afternoon, but time is short, and I certainly don't want to make both of us late. I smile apologetically. "I still haven't decided about the job. I know that's not what you want to hear."

"I'd rather hear that than a definite no!" Louise winks at me. "This means I've still got a chance to persuade you. And listen, if we're both going to the same place, why don't we travel together? I have a cab waiting."

I grab my keys, slide my purse up my shoulder, and slipped my arm through hers.

"Well, in that case, let's arrive in style!"

The street is littered with cars arriving, departing, or parking up, so Louise gets our friendly taxi driver to stop a little way away from the mansion and we make our final approach on foot. My heart begins to beat a little uncomfortably in my chest. I've been to plenty of fancy parties in my life but I seem to recall my invitation was just verbal, and even then only as an afterthought. I hope I'm not about to be turned away at the front door.

"You look nervous," Louise says, tugging on my arm. "Come on! This will be fun!" She catches my eye and laughs. "Well, okay. Maybe not fun. But it's nice to have an excuse to get all dressed up for once. And whatever else I might think of Jessica Patterson, she certainly knows how to throw a party!"

There's no arguing with that, and we pick our way up the long drive, pausing to exchange greetings with people that we pass.

As we make our way into the house, I realize I needn't have worried about being turned away. There are so many people here that I doubt Jessica is even going to see me in the first place. Louise snaps straight into networking mode, and I feel her grip on my arm relax. I take a step back, not wanting to cramp her style and go in search of a drink. If I'm going to be here, I might as well enjoy myself. I see a few neighbors I know and exchange pleasantries with a few more when I catch sight of the angry stranger from earlier that day. He still looks angry, and I see him lurking in the shadows, just waiting to accuse some other hapless elderly person of theft. I make a mental note to steer clear of him and spy a waiter brandishing a tray full of sparkling glasses of champagne. I take one and thank him, and he winks at me and wishes me a good evening. I frown. There's something very familiar about the sandy-haired young man, and I turn to the neighbor I'm standing with to ask if she recognizes him too. But when I look back, he's disappeared.

"Cassie!" Louise is waving at me from across the room, and I go to join her, wishing I had picked up a second glass for my friend until I see she's already holding one.

"It's busy tonight!" I say, marveling at the crowds of people. I'm not sure I've ever seen the population of Patterson looking so well turned out.

"I know!" Louise sighs, sadly. "It'll be our last chance for a night like this for a while."

"What do you mean?"

"You haven't heard?" Louise drops her voice to a whisper and I bend my head close enough to hear. "Jessica is moving out. I guess she'll be selling this house and whatever else she has in Patterson." Her lips quirk. "Rumour is that the bulk of Ed's assets went to a mysterious unnamed benefactor in his will. Jessica Patterson got nothing. Well, very little." She drops her voice, speaking as if only to herself. "Which might explain why she's been dodging my calls lately. She promised a fairly hefty donation to help get Serenity Suites up and running but it looks like that's not going to happen." She shakes her head and forces a smile. "But it's fine. Once I get my first few residents in, things will pick up." She looks at me, her eyes sparkling mischievously. "Especially once I have my new lifestyle manager on board."

I take a long sip of my champagne, thinking over what Louise just said. It ties in with Jessica's excuses earlier. She couldn't help me with my eviction problem, not because she didn't care, but because she really couldn't. Whoever inherited the bulk of Ed Patterson's estate inherited my house along with it. If this mysterious stranger wants to bulldoze the lot and start over, there is not a single thing I can do to stop him. Louise's offer, the job, the accommodation, is the literal lifeline I need. I may not want to take this job, but I think I'm going to have to.

"You're sure you think I can do this job?" I ask her. "And there's a suite with my name on it?"

"Absolutely! You'll get your pick of the place." Louise is looking at me very carefully. "Does this mean what I think it means?"

I clink my champagne glass against hers.

"I think, my friend, you have found yourself a manager."

• • • •

JESSICA HADN'T BEEN kidding when she said that everyone was going to be at tonight's party. I see familiar face after familiar face, and once I make my way through the crowded hallway and find my way towards the kitchen I register I haven't seen our hostess anywhere.

"Hi, Cassie! Great turnout tonight, isn't it?"

I walk past Richard Donovan, another of Patterson's stalwarts, who has a glass of champagne in one hand and a plate piled high with food.

"It certainly looks like everyone's here. What's the occasion?"

"Does there need to be an occasion?" He grins, looking very red-faced and merry and I wonder just how many free drinks he's already helped himself to. "Maybe it's a fond farewell to Patterson." He shoves a chip into his mouth and keeps talking. "Not much keeping Jessica in town now that the old man's gone, is there?"

"But he died months ago!" I protest, wondering what has prompted Jessica to suddenly decide to wrap up her life here. "And she was living here before they got together." I hesitate, trying to remember. "Wasn't she?"

"Don't know. Don't much care." He shovels more food into his mouth and chews noisily. "I'll miss these shindigs, though, if she's leaving town. Maybe you can convince her to stay when you find her."

"Me?" I can't imagine my powers of persuasion will amount to much where Jessica Patterson is concerned.

"She was looking for you earlier." Richard is serious all at once, his forehead wrinkling as he searches his memory. "Asked if I'd seen you. I said I'd keep an eye out."

"Well, now you have seen me." I'm getting a little impatient. What on earth could Jessica have to say to me? "Where is she?"

He shrugs his shoulders, giving me a vaguely apologetic smile, and melts into the crowd. I'm irritated, but not surprised. Most people are only here to socialize and eat someone else's food. I feel a stab of guilt that it's the parties and not the person people will miss if Jessica Patterson does decide to leave.

Now I know she's looking for me, I'm a woman on a mission. Curiosity fires within me and I scan the room, desperate for a glimpse of those model-perfect blonde curls. I see just about every other hair color and style there is except the one I'm looking for and decide to keep moving. The kitchen is a hive of activity and I squeeze past uniformed serving staff, jumping back at the shout that comes from behind the stove.

"Mindy?"

Mindy - my friend, and one-time owner of this kitchen - is slaving away in it again, preparing and serving food for her nemesis.

"What are you doing here?"

"Working." She recovers her shock quicker than I do and hastily shoves two more plates of entrees toward the waiting servers. "What are you doing here?"

"Looking for someone," I say, vaguely. I can't believe she's here tonight. "Did Jessica hire you to cater for this?"

"She did." Mindy offers me a tight-lipped smile. "But she didn't have much choice. My competition backed out at the last minute." She shrugged. "And who am I to refuse a paying customer? Especially when I get to set my own prices." She winks at me. "Are you hungry? Want me to make you a plate?"

"Maybe in a little while." I see her face fall and hastily compliment her on the food. "Everything looks delicious, and I can tell it's going down a treat out there. I'd better keep moving. But if you have a break later, find me, ok?" The last thing I want to think about is my friend prowling the corridors of the house that was once her home, at least not without me for company.

"Will do!" she chirrups and sends me on my way with a wave that's code for *get out of my kitchen before you disrupt anything else* and I take the hint.

There's a staircase through the other kitchen door and I peer up it, trying to work out whether the party has moved to the first floor yet or not. I hear voices, and my feet move almost of their own volition, following the sound of what looks to be a pretty major argument. I remember Mr. Tall Dark and Brooding from downstairs and take the stairs two at a time, ready to come to Jessica's rescue for a second time that day if she needs me to.

"I don't know what you expect me to do about that. It's not my problem."

"You don't understand! Ed was fully supportive of this plan. You know how things were between us, what he was to me. He promised me his full support - that means financing, and - oh!"

I burst into an elegant bedroom and see Jessica facing off, not against a man, but a woman, and a woman I recognize.

"Louise?"

"Cassie!" My friend recovers her composure in record time. "I was just telling Jessica about the newest Serenity Suites news." I must look a little confused because she spells it out. "That you've agreed to come and work for us."

"Oh. Yes." I smile. "At least on a short-term basis."

"Short-term that I hope will become long-term once you get your feet under the table." Louise dances across the room and throws an arm around me. "I couldn't ask for a better manager."

"I haven't done anything yet," I remind her. "And if things don't get a move on I'm going to be *managing* a building site."

"Right. Which is what I was explaining to Jessica, here. I was hoping she could release some more funds..."

"And I told you you're asking the wrong person." Jessica snaps. "Now, if you'll kindly leave me alone, I was in the middle of something when you barged in here."

"Sorry." Louise shoots me a look, and together we slip out into the corridor. "I don't know why she bothered throwing this party if she's going to spend all night hiding in her room," she says, as she drags me back down the stairs and towards the rest of the party-goers. "Like I said to you, she's no help at all with funding. I wasn't even asking for much. A loan, more than anything."

"I thought you said she didn't inherit the bulk of the estate."

"She didn't. But that's property and investments. Ready cash...that goes straight to the spouse." She sniffed. "Ed was always too good for that shrew."

"Louise!"

"Oh, come on. You know he was a much nicer person, and Patterson was a much better town, when he was still married to Mindy. Since Jessica came here she's wrought nothing but destruction on this town and everyone who lives here."

I can't argue with that, and from the pinched look on Louise's face, she won't even listen if I do.

"Come on," I say, sliding my arm through hers and tugging her along with me. "Let's get something to eat. She might be a shrew, and an antisocial one to boot, but I have it on very good authority that the food is pretty good. And I don't know about you but I'm starving."

· · · ·

THE PARTY IS STILL in full swing hours later, and I check my watch before making my way back to the kitchen in search of Mindy. If I'm starting to flag she must be exhausted, not to mention dealing with the additional emotional toll of being back in this house again. No matter how fine she likes to pretend she is, I know my friend, and I'm determined to let her vent if she needs to.

"Mindy! Isn't it about time you took a break?" I sing out as I enter the kitchen, which is just as busy as ever, but despite all the bustling servers I see no sign of my friend. I grab hold of one of them who looks like he can't be any older than sixteen. "Where's Min?"

"On a break." He stares at me wide-eyed, as if fearing a telling-off. I imagine he's had more than a few from Mindy tonight. "Everything's done, we're just serving the last few bits and pieces." He gestures to the sink and I see four people rushing to soak, stack the dishwasher, and restore order to the chaotic kitchen.

"Oh." I feel a little stung that Mindy didn't come to find me and check my phone. There's no sign she tried to call me either. Fighting my disappointment, and trying not to feel too concerned, I slip out of the kitchen through a pair of elegant French windows onto the dimly-lit patio. A few other people have had the same idea, and I gingerly pass couples and groups talking in low, intimate whispers, making my way around the side of the house to an overgrown patch of earth I recognize as Mindy's herb garden. At least, it used to be an herb garden. Now it looks like the only things being cultivated are weeds, and I sigh ruefully as I look down at this small patch of earth that was once my old friend's pride and joy. *It's probably for the best that she's not here with me to see it*, I think, stepping lightly through the overgrowth and continuing my lap of the house. I don't know how Mindy does it, continuing to live in the same town as her ex-husband. Mind you, it's not like she doesn't have a right to stay here. Mindy and Ed were the power couple of Patterson when they were together, and she's just as much a force of nature in the town without him as she was with him, maybe more so.

I hear raised voices ahead and am sure I recognize one of them, at least. I increase my pace, rushing around the side of the house but there's nobody there, and for a minute I wonder if I'm going mad. Maybe I imagined the voices. Then a scream catches my attention and I look up just in time to see a shadowy figure clinging to the edge of the balcony.

"Help!" Jessica squeals. "Someone!" Her words are shrill and indistinct. "Someone help me!"

I'm pinned in place, not sure what to do, and see a dark shadow rush past me towards the balcony but it's too late. With one last desperate scream, Jessica's grip loosens. She reaches out to grasp at nothing but air and then plummets, landing with a sickening thud on the empty patio beneath.

Chapter Six

A dark cloud settles over Patterson that week, in more ways than one. When I wake up the next morning, I can hear the rain drilling on my roof, and it takes me a while to get up to face the day. I'm feeling melancholy as I move around my little house, wondering how many mornings like this I will have to spend here.

It can't be helped, I tell myself. *And at least now you have somewhere to go.* I decide I'd better make my way to the Serenity Suites site that day. I want to see Louise again and learn a little bit more about the job I've accepted. It might be necessity, rather than choice, that has me working there, but Louise certainly seems to think I'll be a good fit for the role. I want to see if I agree with her assessment. And I'd like to learn a little bit more about where I'm going to be living. I doubt I'll be able to take all this furniture with me, so I need to start making some decisions.

First things first. Breakfast. Nothing in my kitchen seems particularly appealing, and I decide if ever there was a day that cake for breakfast was an acceptable alternative, it's the morning after a murder. I pick up my umbrella, slide my purse onto my arm, and trot out of my house and into the rain, planning to stop in at Mindy's for a coffee and a pastry on my way to Serenity Suites. The café is busy, which doesn't surprise me. On days like today when it's raining people tend to take up residence, and as I step inside the crowded building, I hear more than one hushed conversation fall silent. On days like today when it's raining, *and when there's a scandal to discuss.*

"Cassie!" Samuel Greenwood waves at me from his usual seat and beckons me over to join him. Normally I might hesitate, but there aren't exactly many other options. I ought to be grateful to have the chance to sit down, and I obediently make for his table.

"Just in time to help me finish the crossword," he says, angling the newspaper towards me. I'm surprised at how normal he seems. Maybe he hasn't heard what's happened yet.

"Seventeen down," he says, taking a slow sip of his coffee. "Five letters. Excuse."

I frown, then look at the puzzle, trying to locate the space he's talking about.

"Alibi," he says, letting out a throaty laugh. "Just my little joke." He taps the crossword puzzle. "I certainly wouldn't expect you to focus on something like this, not with everything else that is going on. So come on, tell me all about it. You were there, weren't you? Or, let me guess, you were in the bathroom when it happened." He rolls his eyes. "That always happens to me. If something exciting is going on, you can guarantee it will happen at the very moment I step out of the room."

I smile but say nothing, not quite sure where to begin.

"I wasn't at the party, of course. Had an invite, and everything!" Samuel sighs. "I'm not one for getting dressed up and dancing, and I never did care for that Jessica woman, so I stayed home and had a quiet evening in. Regretting it now!" He seems to notice at last I am not matching his jocular tone and grows serious. "Was it horrible?"

"No," I admit with a sigh. "It was just what you'd imagine a Jessica Patterson party to be. Extravagant, over-the-top, crowded." I smile sadly. "I don't think any of us had any idea how the night would end."

"Maybe she planned it that way."

I frown, looking at Samuel in confusion.

"Well, if there's one way to go out with a bang it's with a house full of people. You know Jessica. She was never one to do anything without an audience."

I try to process this, putting my thoughts tentatively into words.

"You think Jessica killed herself?"

Samuel shrugs his shoulders.

"Maybe. Maybe not. A lot of people are saying it was accidental, but I've been to that house. The only way she could have accidentally fallen off a balcony was if she was balancing on the edge of the railing. Nobody in their right mind would do that."

"Right."

"So come on, then. What's your view? Did she jump? Did she fall? Was she pushed?" He smiles grimly at this last comment, and I'm not sure if he wants to know my answer. I'm saved from giving it because a slight hush falls over the café as the door to the kitchen swings open and Mindy slips through it. My friend looks surprisingly chipper, considering everything that happened the previous evening. I make my excuses to Samuel and drift over to the counter to place my order.

"Morning, Min," I say, with a cautious smile. "How are you holding up?"

"Holding up?" She beams at me. "Business is better than ever! Nothing like a good dose of scandal to get people talking.

And where else are people going to sit around and talk than in here?" She seems to notice that it's me for the first time, but her smile doesn't dim. "Your usual? How about something sweet? I've just made some fresh croissants."

"Sounds good," I say. Mindy bustles away, whistling a happy little tune as she slips back into the kitchen to put my order together. My frown darkens. If I didn't know my friend better I might say she was happy.

And why shouldn't she be? An insidious little voice asks in the back of my mind. *It's not like she and Jessica were what you might call friends. They hated each other.* I bite my lip. But that doesn't mean Mindy would have had a hand in killing her, would it?

I get my coffee order to go, and wave goodbye to Samuel as I make my way out of the café and down the road to the Serenity Suites building site. It's a little more subdued than yesterday but indoors away from the rain there are just as many workmen busily wrangling the site into shape. I stop the first person I see and ask if he knows where Louise is. He gestures along the main corridor and I follow his lead, picking my way carefully through the detritus and stopping only when I see three other workmen standing around not working. No, I realize, being kept from their work by a fourth man. Joe has one hand on the ladder the workmen brandish and looks as if he's trying to talk himself onto their crew. I tap him lightly on the shoulder and he turns, his manner shifting as he notices me.

"What do you want?"

What a charmer. Still, if I'm going to work here, I'm going to have to learn to get on with people like this.

"Good morning, Joe," I say brightly and thrust my croissant at him. "Thought you might like a treat."

"Well, thank you very much, Cally," he says, lifting the pastry out of its paper bag and eating half of it in one large bite. The workmen scatter, eager to get back to their jobs, and I decide I can spare five minutes to speak to Serenity Suites' first and so far only resident. After all, it looks like we going to be neighbors before very much longer.

"It's Cassie," I say tiredly, running a hand through my hair and wincing as a trickle of rainwater finds its way down my neck.

"You look awful," Joe says, narrowly avoiding spraying me with crumbs. "Didn't you sleep well?"

"Not very." I take a pointed sip of my coffee and glare at him. I know there are bags under my eyes, and I'm sure I've certainly looked better, but he doesn't have to mention it.

"So what kept you up all night? Hot date?" He waggles his eyebrows at me and I grimace.

"I was at a party."

"Oh, even better." He polishes off the last of the pastry and hands the bag back to me. "Hang on, was this the same party that Louise was at? She looks like hell too, and I've barely seen her all morning."

"That's because some of us have to work," I point out.

"I worked plenty," Joe says. He runs a hand through his thinning, gray hair. "Wish I still was, if you really want to know. This sort of place can drive a man crazy. So anyway, tell me about this party. Anything exciting happen?"

I open my mouth to say no, then think better of it. I certainly don't want to rehash the whole murder thing with this man I barely know, but something inside me prompts me not to lie.

"Something happened," I allow. "But that's not why I'm here. I need to speak to Louise about something else altogether."

"About you moving in." Joe grins at me. "About you taking the job as general manager here?"

"How did you know about that?" I frown, annoyed that Louise has been sharing all my pertinent details with anyone who will listen. "And it's *lifestyle manager*."

"I have my sources." Joe winks. "Frankly, I think she could do better."

"You don't even know me!" I point out. "And it's not like there are hundreds of other people champing at the bit to come and work here." I roll my eyes at him. "I can't imagine why not."

That only seems to amuse him, and his grin widens.

"Just wait till the rest of these apartments are filled, Cassie. You're going to have your hands full keeping us happy. Well, top of the morning." He salutes me and turns to walk away. He doesn't make it far before he catches sight of the rain, still falling in sheets outside. He turns around and salutes again. "Guess I'll get my steps in with a lap of the building," he says, and strolls off, whistling to himself as he goes.

I carry on my way to Louise's office, wondering if I ought to walk back my acceptance of the job. Then I remember I don't exactly have a lot of other options. *Besides,* I tell myself. *I can handle Joe.*

Chapter Seven

Louise's office seems even smaller than I remember it and when I open the door she's hunched over her desk, tapping furiously into her computer.

"Bad time?" I ask when she lifts her head. The dark scowl she was wearing recedes as she notices me and she beckons me swiftly inside.

"Not at all." She smiles. "I'm glad you're here. I need to talk to you."

"About the job?" I frown at the way Louise's smile slips. "Have you changed your mind about me coming to work here?" My temporary contentment begins to fade. Here was me thinking I was the only one wavering about accepting the job at Serenity Suites. Had Louise found someone else? "I thought we agreed last night...I mean, if you don't want me -"

"Of course I want you!" Louise is her sunny, capable self again. "You just caught me off-guard. To be honest I haven't been able to concentrate on a thing today, not after..."

"Right." I swallow the last of my coffee and hang onto the cup, picking at its cardboard sleeve. Jessica's death, in such a horrible manner, and so publicly, has to have upset a lot of people. *Even if they didn't like her very much to begin with.*

"But let's not dwell on that anymore." Louise taps a few more buttons on her keyboard then leans over her desk, fixing me with a smile that is almost her old, mischievous self. "How would you like to see your new home?"

. . . .

THE APARTMENT SHE'S picked out for me isn't quite finished - the floor is still bare and I can see patches of spackle on the wall that haven't been painted over yet - but it's not bad. I can picture where some of my furniture would go, and the rest...well, there's nothing like downsizing to let go of a few relics from the past.

"You'll have access to a little private patio through the glass doors here," Louise continues, leading me across the room. "The rooms on the first and second floors have balconies, but I hope -" She pauses before looking at me, and I realize I let out a little gasp almost without realizing it. "Cassie?" I hear Jessica Patterson's voice echoing in my mind and close my eyes, praying for the moment to pass. *Someone! Someone help me!* "Maybe this is a little too soon...."

"No." I force myself to smile. "I'm fine. And this place is lovely." There's a muffled shout as workmen elsewhere in the building start up the whirr of a power drill and I grimace. "Or it will be when it's finished."

There's a knock at my open door and both Louise and I turn towards it. I'm startled to see a tall, dark-haired figure I notice.

"Oh!" Louise jumps away from me, glancing at her watch. "Am I late?"

"I'm early." The man smiles, and I'm caught off-guard, thinking it's the first time I've seen Patterson's resident Grump wearing anything other than a scowl. "And you're busy."

"Not very." Louise turns back to me. "How about I let you look around a bit more, Cassie? I have a meeting but feel free to stay here as long as you like. Take any measurements you need, and if you have any questions that the workmen can't answer, you know where to find me." She lays a comforting arm on my shoulder, then turns back to the new arrival. Her posture shifts, and she slides into professional mode as she steers him towards her office. I'm left alone, but the ripple of eager anticipation I'd felt on first seeing my soon-to-be new home fades into suspicion. Since when did those two know each other? I debate my course of action for all of a minute before trotting after them, fabricating some kind of reason to call out after my friend.

"Louise?"

She and Mr. Tall-Dark-and-Grumpy have already turned a corner and she doesn't hear me, but somebody else does. I feel my good mood sink even further when Joe comes whistling down the corridor.

"Are you still here?"

"Are you?" I fire back. It's too late to catch up to Louise now. With a sigh, I turn on my heel and stalk back to my soon-to-be apartment, not entirely surprised when Joe walks with me.

"So, when are you going to be moving in? It's a room-and-board kind of deal, isn't it?"

"Isn't what?" I sound tired and try to inject a bit of good humor into my words with a smile. "Oh, the lifestyle manager job?"

"Lifestyle manager." I can practically hear the air quotes Joe puts around my new job title. "What does that mean, anyway?"

"I have no idea," I confess, stopping at my door. "But Louise seems to think I'm perfect for the job, so..."

"You can't be any worse than the last person she tried to hire for it, anyway." Joe peers over my shoulder, trying to see into the room, and I let it swing closed again before he can see through more than a three-inch gap.

"What last person?" I turn to look at him properly. "What are you talking about?"

"Oh, nothing." Joe's smile is too quick and too wide to be even the least bit convincing.

"I know she had someone else lined up, but that fell through."

"Which works out well for you, doesn't it?" Joe winks. "Louise thinks you're perfect for the job. Or you will be, once there are enough of us living here to require -" He clears his throat and I think he might be stifling a laugh. "Lifestyle management." He starts to walk down the corridor, waving as he goes, and I hear the first few bars of an old hymn as he resumes his whistling, but the melody leaves me feeling a little confused, and a lot less enthusiastic about this situation than I was a few minutes ago. *Who else did Teresa ask to take this job?* I wonder. *And what made them say no?*

· · · ·

I SOON GET THE MEASURE of my new home, and once I've taken a few photos and made a few notes on my phone, I'm kind of at a loose end. I think of heading back out the way I came in but the thought of running into Joe again makes me rethink that plan, and after a little jimmying the lock of the glass doors I manage to stumble out of them and into the gardens. The rain has stopped, and I take that as a sign to go exploring. My private patio is little more than a few square feet of dusty cobbles, but I can already picture making it my own little piece of Eden. A few potted plants and a nice comfy lawn chair will make it feel like home in no time at all. I inelegantly manage to climb over the low fence into the wider grounds and look around with an eye to my future career. *Lifestyle manager.* When Louise first told me about the job she sold it as an admin position, a glorified RA, only my charges would be retirees instead of college kids. Now, after my latest run-in with Joe, I wonder if a gaggle of old people will be more or less work to manage than a bunch of teenagers. *More*, I think, surveying the rolling gardens with a grimace. *Definitely more.*

There's a thud from behind me and I turn around, looking up just in time to see a shadow pass across the balcony above. My heart leaps into my throat and I'm reminded of the awful event I witnessed last evening. Then, just in time for me to really think I'm going mad, I hear a shout. My eyes go straight back to the balcony, but even as I blink I can see it's empty, and I notice the shout didn't come from there at all, but somewhere else. I follow the sound, walking through an arch of ivy until I see Louise arguing with one of Patterson's enthusiastic young deputies as Sheriff Bob Cooper and the dark-haired stranger stand by watching.

"Please don't make this any more difficult than it already is, Ma'am," the deputy pleads, his voice cracking as he tries to assert his non-existent authority.

"It's just a few questions, Louise. You can't object to a few questions, surely?"

"I can object to you dragging me out of my place of work to answer them," Louise hisses, reddening as she looks around at the small crowd of curious workmen pretending not to watch her resisting arrest. She catches sight of me and beckons me over to join them. "Tell them, Cassie! You were with me at the party, weren't you? There, see! I have an alibi."

"Yes, I was with her," I say, striding forward to help my friend. "What seems to be the problem, Deputy?" I can hear the grandmotherly tone in my voice and cringe, then decide age and infirmity might work in my favor. I lean heavily on one side, pretending I have a limp, and smile wearily at the young man. "Surely we can sort this out quite easily inside." I let out an exhausted sigh. "Where we can sit down."

"Sorry, Ms. Clinton." Sheriff Cooper steps forward, exchanging a look with the dark-haired stranger that, if I didn't know any better, I'd think was one of amusement. I blink, and their faces are both neutral once more. "Louise, you'll have to come with us to the station. It'll only take a few minutes." He glances at the stranger. "Your lawyer can accompany you."

"I'm not -"

"He's not -"

They scramble to provide an answer and I'm not the only one curious to hear who exactly this man is and what he and Louise have been discussing, but before anyone else can say a word, a shrill, demanding voice echoes across the gardens.

"Ms. Hamilton? Louise? What on earth is going on here?"

Chapter Eight

Mrs. Ophelia Roy is not the sort of person to be easily brushed off, and when Louise looks helplessly in my direction I know this is my cue. I might be stepping into my lifestyle manager position sooner than I'd like, but if ever there was a moment to prove to myself - and everyone else - what I can do, it's now.

"Good afternoon!" I say, as brightly as I can. "Can I be of any assistance?"

Mrs. Roy slides her glasses down her nose and peers over them at me.

"I'm Cassie. Cassie Clinton. I'm the new lifestyle manager here at Serenity Suites." I glance at Louise. "Or I will be."

This introduction seems to offer Louise enough of a lifeline to catch hold of, and she jumps in to introduce us properly.

"Cassie! Yes, this is Mrs. Roy. She's another soon-to-be resident here although I don't believe you were scheduled to be moving in quite yet..."

"Certainly not! All this dust and activity is not at all good for my constitution." She gives a little cough, before glaring accusingly at the gentlemen present as if they, and their entire gender, are responsible for her discomfort. "I only came to clarify a few details with you, Louise, dear, but it looks as if you're a little too busy at the moment." She sweeps an imperious gaze around the group before coming to rest on me. "I suppose your assistant will be able to help me."

I bristle at the term *assistant*, and the healthy dose of skepticism that comes along with it, but then I remember the fearful shadow on Louise's face and decide I'm more than happy to endure a little condescension if it helps my friend's new business. Helping Serenity Suites will help me too in the long run.

"I'd be more than happy to." I lay a light hand on Mrs. Roy's back and steer her towards the main property. "Let's step inside, shall we?"

"Oh, Cassie! You can use my office," Louise says, her voice ringing with polite desperation. I nod, vaguely wondering where else I could have taken Mrs. Roy that doesn't still look like a building site.

"So! Do you often have visits from law enforcement?"

We pass a contractor whistling and wearing his hard hat at a jaunty - and entirely impractical - angle and one sharp look from Mrs. Roy is enough to put a stop to that. Two others see us coming and scurry out of our way and I begin to wonder just what I've signed up for in offering to take our newest arrival off Louise's hands.

"Here we are!" I feign enthusiasm I don't feel as I reach the door to Louise's office and push it open, immediately seeing the chaos within and closing the door on it again before Mrs. Roy can cross the threshold. "I have a better idea! There is still so much work going on here at the moment that it's so loud and - and dusty, as you said." I pause and mimic Mrs. Roy's earlier cough. "I'm sure we can find somewhere a little more comfortable for us to have a catch-up. You look like a lady with impeccable taste. Perhaps you'll join me in a pot of tea?"

· · · ·

"WHO IS THAT?"

Having settled Mrs. Roy comfortably at a table in the window so she can get a feel for the bustling, friendly center of Patterson, I'm taking a moment to myself while I order our drinks. Mindy's cafe was my first - and only - idea of where to take my new friend. I'm just relieved there was a break in the weather long enough for us to reach it without getting rained on.

"A new Serenity Suites resident." I wince. "Or a prospective resident, at least. I'm trying to seal the deal."

"And you thought bringing her here would do that?" I can picture the incredulous eyebrow raise on Min's face without having to look at her.

"Well, there wasn't anywhere we could sit and talk there. It's still half under construction. And with the sheriff..." I trail off, catching a curious glint in Mindy's eyes. "I thought we'd come here for refreshments. It can't hurt." I offer her a pleading smile. "Especially if you throw in a couple of those beautiful strawberry shortcake desserts with our pot of tea."

"This is a coffee shop," Mindy grumbles, as she good-naturedly fulfills my request. "You know. Coffee. That goes just as well with strawberry shortcake as anything."

"Of course it does." I'm trying to placate Mindy without undoing all my good work with Mrs. Roy, who, it seems, is nothing if not particular. "But I promised tea and if I can't even deliver on that..."

"Fine." Mindy reaches across the counter to place a heavy teapot down with a thud on a tray, and I catch sight of something glinting on her wrist.

"Ooh, is that new?" Like a magpie I reach for it, and Min jerks her hand back, then laughs, awkwardly sliding her cuff down over a delicate rose-gold watch.

"You startled me!" She shakes her head. "It's not new. It's something of an heirloom, but I only just decided to start wearing it." She pats the watch surreptitiously. "You only live once, you know?"

"That's right." I reach for the tray and lift it, straining a little under the weight. "You're welcome to join us if you aren't too busy."

"Don't you have important Serenity Suites business to discuss?"

I shake my head, then smile, hoping I don't look quite as desperate as I feel.

"It's more about giving Mrs. Roy a good impression of the town. She's going to be moving down to Patterson from Coleridge Bay, and I want her to see what a great place this is to live in."

"Right." Mindy doesn't sound all that convinced. "You mean, apart from the crushing poverty and occasional murder?" I whip my head around to look at her and she smiles. "Only joking. You know I love this town as much as the next person." She sighs. "And a lot more than most." A movement in the window catches her eye and she waves, but when I look, whoever she greeted has long gone. Something seems to have cheered her up, though, because she hurries around the counter to join me and heaves the teapot off my tray, making my whole load a lot lighter. "You know I'd never speak ill of the dead, Cassie, but I have a feeling that things might just change a bit around here in the wake of *that woman*'s demise." She's smiling as she crosses the cafe to my table and I hurry to keep up, wondering what has happened to alter my friend's mood so swiftly and completely, and hoping that it has a contagious effect on Mrs. Ophelia Roy, who could use a little cheer.

"Here we are!" I carefully settle the tray in the middle of our table and pull up another chair. "I hope you don't mind, I invited Mindy to join us. She is a Patterson legend, and I'm sure will be able to answer any questions you might have about the town."

"You work here?" There's something almost dismissive about Mrs. Roy's tone, but I'm not going to let a little thing like arrogance deter me.

"Mindy owns the cafe outright. She's the best baker in town." I pass the largest of our two strawberry shortcakes to Ophelia. "These are to die for."

"I hope not!" Ophelia lifts the cake to her lips and takes a dainty bite, chewing and swallowing before allowing a smile that transforms her entire countenance. "Goodness, you weren't kidding! Absolutely divine. My dear - Mandy, was it?"

"Mindy," Min says, exchanging a look with me as she pours two cups of tea and allows our new friend to fawn a little over just how good her baking is.

"I don't think I've tasted shortbread this perfect since I was last in Edinburgh. Do you know Scotland?"

"I've heard of it." I hear the laughter in Mindy's voice and decide that she has certainly been my secret weapon in getting Ophelia on my side. I slide off my chair and hurry across the quiet cafe to fetch a third cup and saucer that will hopefully persuade Mindy to stay put and work her magic a little longer.

I wave at Samuel as I pass him and he barely looks up from the crossword he's frowning over. I wonder if he's annoyed at how quickly I ditched him this morning, and decide I'd better put some effort in if I want to keep him as a friend. *But only a friend*, I remind myself. *So not too much effort*. I certainly don't want anyone to get any wires crossed.

"So, Mindy." I can hear the businesslike tone in Ophelia's voice as I return to our table and am ready to back my friend up on whatever she needs. But Ophelia's next words are enough to stop me in my tracks. "Who do you think is responsible for this dreadful murder at the mansion?"

I'm so startled I almost drop the cup and saucer I'm carrying and it clatters noisily onto the table, making everyone jump.

"Sorry!" I can hear the overly false note in my voice and pray it's not so grating to everybody else. "More tea? I thought you might like to join us, Min. Here, shall I pour?" I'm chattering away, hoping and praying it'll be enough of a distraction to turn the conversation in a new direction. But I have underestimated the ability of Mrs. Ophelia Roy to get what she wants.

"I have no idea." Mindy's gaze is fixed on the window and she fusses absent-mindedly with her watch.

"Neither do I," I say, hastily taking a sip of my tea. "Well, this is pleasant. And just think, Mrs. Roy, you can become a regular customer at the cafe once you're all moved in at Serenity Suites. That's if you don't want to take advantage of the fully stocked dining area on-site..."

"I suppose it might cause quite a scandal," Ophelia continues, wetting her lips in anticipation. "If the manager of Serenity Suites is declared to be a suspect."

"Who?" Mindy snaps to attention.

"Sheriff Cooper asked Louise to accompany him to the station," I say in a low voice. "But just to answer a few questions. He'll be taking statements off everybody soon enough."

"I'm amazed you've avoided him for this long," Mindy says, reaching across me for my untouched strawberry shortcake and breaking off a piece to nibble. "I know Deputy Davis spoke to you at the time, but -"

"Were you there?" Ophelia is all interest, her pride and superiority replaced with craven curiosity. "Did you see anything?"

"Cassie saw everything." Mindy sighs. "I'm sure her testimony is going to be the thing to solve it. When Sheriff Cooper came to speak to me I was no help at all. I spent all evening slaving away in the kitchen." I turn my head at this, remembering distinctly that Mindy had been nowhere to be found when I'd gone looking for her only minutes before Jessica's fall. "I suppose I should be grateful to have such a rock-solid alibi." She shivers, toying with her watch again. "After all, I'm sure as far as some people are concerned I have more motive to want that woman dead than anyone. But I was busy in the kitchen the whole time."

Chapter Nine

"You were outside when the, ah, incident took place?"

The young deputy taking my statement looks to be about twelve years old. I'm sure I know his name. Dylan, or Ryan? Something like that. And he has a sister...

"Ms. Clifton?"

Dylan, or Ryan, whatever his name is, is looking at me wide-eyed and terrified that my mild distraction is a sign of some deeper trauma that is about to manifest itself physically.

"I was outside," I say, smiling a little to try and reassure the poor young man that I'm not about to keel over and die myself. "I wanted some fresh air. It was so crowded indoors, and so noisy!" I stop, worried that that complaint makes me sound even older than I am. "Well, anyway. I was outside. I heard a scream. I looked up, and there she was. Hanging from the edge of the balcony." I shudder, remembering the site of Jessica Patterson dangling from the edge of the ornamental railings.

"I see. And was anyone there with her? Anybody else you could see?"

"Well, I imagine there must have been. She didn't climb over the edge herself."

My voice must sound a little bit sterner than I mean it to. Dylan or Ryan doesn't reply at first, and I see him catch the eye of someone in the doorway of the small interrogation room. I'm not surprised when Sheriff Bob Cooper steps in and takes over.

"Good afternoon, Cassie!" He pats me warmly on the arm. "Nice to see you again, although I'm very sorry about the circumstances, of course. Dylan, go and fetch Ms. Clifton a cup of sweet, hot tea, will you? Lots of sugar. For the shock."

"I'm fine," I protest, but then I decide that if I'm going to be kept here against my will and forced to re-issue a statement I already gave I might as well have some refreshments while I do so. "Thank you, young man." I cringe at that. Young man? I'm becoming my mother.

"Now, Cassie."

"Now, Sheriff Cooper." I meet his gaze without backing down. "Why, exactly, am I here?"

I had finally managed to persuade Ophelia Roy in favor of Serenity Suites and Patterson as a whole, only for all my credulity to be ruined when Deputy Dylan or Ryan or whatever his name is stepped into the cafe and summoned me to the sheriff's station to give a statement of my own. I was only a little relieved to find out that Louise had already been released. *She can take over the charm offensive now,* I think, shifting in my seat. *Because with the triple threat of the murder, the investigation, and the fact that Serenity Suites is still very much under construction, she's going to need to work hard to keep prospective residents on her side.* I try to forget the look of shock and suspicion that rested on Ophelia Roy's face when I last saw her and drag my attention back to the present.

"I don't see why you needed to speak to me again," I say, hearing the note of irritability in my voice and not caring to modulate it. "I already gave my statement on the spot." There's a lump in my throat and I swallow with effort, now grateful I said yes to the promise of a cup of tea. "I told you everything I could at the time."

"You were very helpful." Bob Cooper shuffles some papers together, then folds his hands on top of them and looks at me. "But there are just a few more details we need to clarify."

Clarify. He means "check up on".

"I assure you I was completely truthful in my first statement," I bristle. "I certainly won't be changing my tune now."

"Cassie, relax." Bob smiles at me. "You're not here under any kind of suspicion. I'm sort of hoping you can help me out." He leans across the table towards me, dropping his voice to a confidential whisper. "You may have noticed the deputies here are a little..."

"Young?"

"Inexperienced."

I arch an eyebrow at him.

"I don't have all that much experience around murder myself, Sheriff. This is Patterson, not New York City."

"But you have experience of people," Bob reassures me. "And you know this town better than just about anyone else. People like you and they trust you. And you were right there on the scene. You, Cassie Clinton, are what people might call a prime witness."

It's a long time since I've been called a prime *anything*, and I'm not so inundated with compliments that I can choose to let them slide when they come my way.

"Keep talking," I say, with a wary look.

"There's not much more to say." Bob leans back in his seat, but he leaves his hand flat against his file of notes. "I just wanted to ask you to keep your eyes and ears open as you go about your day."

"Spy on my friends and neighbors, you mean?"

"Certainly not! But if you happen to come across anything of interest...anything that might be useful in solving this crime before -" He stops talking all of a sudden and clears his throat.

Before? Before it happens again? I feel the color drain from my face and glance towards the door, wondering just where my little friend has got to with my now-rather-necessary cup of tea.

"Just let me know if you think of anything," Bob says, patting my arm gently in an awkward effort to reassure me. "There's probably nothing. I know your friend Louise was no help at all. Said she didn't see Mrs. Patterson all night, despite her being the host of the party. Although I gather that was something of a habit at these events. Stuff the house full of guests and there's no way she could spare the time to visit with them all." He looks at me. "You saw her though, didn't you? Before..." He drops his gaze to the file folder, flipping it open and sifting through a few pages until he finds the one he is looking for. "It says here that you spoke to her in her room before she demanded to be left alone."

"That's right." I'm not sure if Bob notices how strangled my voice is, but I certainly do. "I spoke to her." *Along with Louise, who's now denying she was even there!* I frown, thinking that's another loose end I need to tie up with a friend. "Did - did Louise tell you anything else? Anything useful, I mean?" I qualify when the sheriff's brow furrows. "I know you probably can't discuss other people's statements, or share evidence, or..." I smile, trying to wrangle some control of my emotions before I betray both Louise and myself in front of the sheriff who's got so much faith in me he's practically recruiting me to join his team. "I just wondered. It might be helpful to know if there are any other avenues to follow."

"I don't think so." Bob closes the file folder again and smiles at me. "Just keep doing what you do best and let us know if anything of interest comes to light. We'll be busy doing our jobs, too, so you needn't worry. We'll soon get to the bottom of all this." The door to the interrogation room swings open and the young deputy enters clutching a steaming cup of tea that he puts down carefully on the table in front of me.

"Thank you." I take a quick, scalding sip and gag. The poor boy must have dumped half a container of sugar into it but to my surprise it helps, and I begin to feel a bit more human. I take another sip and realize Bob is watching very closely.

"Don't worry, Cassie," he tells me again, with a reassuring smile. "There's still every chance this was just a horrible accident. But if it wasn't, I'll make sure we catch the person responsible just as soon as we can."

I nod but I'm not entirely persuaded. If he and half of Patterson still think Jessica's death was just a tragic accident, then they won't look very hard to find her killer. I saw that poor woman fall. There was nothing accidental about it.

Someone! Someone, help me! Just the memory of her last words sends a shiver up my spine. There was something so pointed about them, as if *someone* was directed - well, at someone specific. *But that's nonsense. If she'd been asking for help she'd have used a name. And why would she ask for help from the very person who put her in the position to need it?* I take another sip of my tea. There's no way Jessica's fall was an accident. And I'm not about to let whoever pushed her get away with it.

Chapter Ten

"**O**oh, Cassie! What treasures have you brought me?"

I laugh at the enthusiasm with which Annabelle receives the first of many boxes I have packed and ready to bring to her store. It's been a quiet few days, at least as far as I'm concerned, but I haven't wasted my time. I've been busily tidying, decluttering, and downsizing the current contents of my house to just a few things I will have space for at Serenity Suites. I'm not a clutter bug by any means, but it hasn't always been easy deciding what to keep and what to get rid of. This box was the first one I filled, and I heave it onto the counter for Annabelle to pick through.

"I don't think you'll find much to treasure in here, I'm afraid! It's mostly just old crockery and kitchen supplies, but they'll make someone very happy, I'm sure." I wipe my hands on my jeans and glance back towards the door. "I've got a few more boxes to bring after this one if you're happy to take them?"

"Of course, dear." Annabelle is bent over my box, counting and pricing things in her head as she reaches inside. "I'm here all afternoon, so you can drop them off any time."

"Thanks." I check my phone, but Louise still hasn't returned my call. I bite my lip, wondering if I can fit in a quick visit in person to Serenity Suites. I've scarcely spoken to her since her interview with Sheriff Cooper, and I want to reassure myself that she's doing ok. It's not like I think she's a real suspect, at least Bob didn't seem to think so. But an ongoing murder investigation isn't the only problem Louise is juggling right now. I wonder if she's made any progress with sourcing some more funding. *Because if not, then all of this is for nothing.* I shake my head. *One crisis at a time, Cassie.* The date for my eviction is looming large in my mind and at least I have somewhere to move to until I hear otherwise. A new house and a new job. That's a lot more than some of my neighbors have right now.

"Do you need anything else, dear?"

Annabelle seems to have noticed I'm standing around, and she looks up from curating my box of kitchen supplies with a gentle smile.

"It's hard to let go sometimes, isn't it?" She reaches into the box and pulls out a rainbow-colored ceramic mug. "Here. Why don't you keep this one?"

I take the mug, and just looking at it makes me smile. This was a gift from one of my favorite nieces. Meredith had bought it for me *just because* and drinking my morning coffee from it does make me feel a little less alone. Maybe it will go just as well in my new home as it has done in my old one.

"Thanks, Annabelle." I head towards the street, pausing in the doorway to wave. "And you're sure you don't mind me dropping off a few other boxes? It might not be right away. I have some jobs to do first."

"Not at all, dear!" Annabelle's smile drops into the tiniest frown and when I hear a tentative throat clearing I notice why. I'm blocking the doorway for someone who wants to get inside.

"Oh, I'm sorry!" I jump aside and let a short, stout, bottle-blonde woman inside. She's clutching a box of her own and I can't help but peek inside as she passes me. "Looks like it's the season for decluttering!" I say, with a smile.

"Huh?" She glares at me, clutching her box a little more tightly as if she worried I was going to take something from it.

"Nothing," I say, waving my rescued mug at Annabelle and leaving her and her new customer to it. I guess not everyone has the time to stand around all afternoon making small talk. *And neither do I*, I remind myself, setting an alarm on my phone that will go off half an hour before the antiques store closes. I've got plenty of time to swing by Serenity Suites and check up on Louise without eating too much into my decluttering time. *I can drop off my first item in my new apartment*, I think, swinging my arms jauntily as I walk down the street. *It's a small start, but it's something that will help the new place feel like home.* I wince, wondering if there's been much progress on the walls-and-floor front, but decide that's another good reason to call in today. I can get a timeframe for my move from Louise and start to organize my bigger items of furniture.

To my surprise, Serenity Suites is looking less like a building site than it did the last time I was there. Or perhaps I'm just getting used to it. I wave and offer a cheery good morning to the workmen who are repainting the sign over the front door and take care to slip inside without any risk of brushing against wet paint this time.

I see Joe deep in conversation with a tall figure whose back is to me, and I hurry on past them, grateful to escape being drawn into another conversation with Serenity Suites' primary resident. I wonder how Joe copes with being the only person to live on-site at the moment, then realize that within a matter of a few days, I'll be joining him. I pick up my pace, taking the route I committed to memory the first time Louise showed me to my room. I'm trusting my memory and not my instincts because just about everything in this corridor looks different - newer, shinier, and much more inviting. There's a little flutter of excitement as I push the door to my apartment but it doesn't yield and I slam against it. I rear back and try again before I'm finally forced to acknowledge the truth: the door is locked. I hesitate for a moment, glancing back over my shoulder to check Joe is still deep in conversation with his new friend, and then I decide to take a circuitous route to Louise's office, hoping she is in and can give me the keys to my soon-to-be home. I haven't got a start date for working here yet or for moving in, but I'm eager to get started and this, at least, is a problem I'll be able to solve. My mind races back to the other problem I've been mulling over whenever I have a spare minute, but I'm making even less progress on solving the murder of Jessica Patterson.

I think back over my last proper interaction with Jessica - the way she had unceremoniously thrown Louise and me out of her room. *Leave me alone, I was in the middle of something when you barged in here.* What had she been in the middle of? Or was it not a *what* but a *who*? Her last words come to mind again. *Someone help me!* And I wonder if there had been time for another bad-tempered interview after we left Jessica, but before she was left dangling from her balcony. Of course there was! Plenty of time. *And plenty of suspects.* I'm still turning over the matter in my mind as I reach Louise's office, but I see her emerge from inside a little ahead of my arrival and pick up my pace, letting all concerns about Jessica Patterson drop in my eagerness to catch up with my friend.

"Louise!"

She hasn't heard me: she's distracted, and I watch in frustration as she disappears around the corner too fast for me to catch her. I hesitate for a moment, debating whether to follow her or not, but then I see the door to her office is still open. I slip inside, certain I'll be able to easily lay my hand on the keys I'm looking for. I'm sure she meant to give me my own set before now, anyway.

Louise's office is just as chaotic as it's always been, and I quickly survey the chaos of papers that cover the surface of the desk. I don't mean to read them, but one page leaps out to me when I see my name, and I skim over it quickly, seeing it's a contract of employment. There's a space above my name indicating the need for a signature and I grab a pen and hurriedly scribble my name, before checking Louise has already done the same. *Simone Louise Hamilton*. I frown. *Simone?* I always thought Louise was her first name, but she opts to use her middle name. *That's not so very unusual*, I think. *I can't remember the last person to call me* Cassandra, *after all*. I slide the signed contract to the very top of the pile, making sure Louise will see it when she comes back to the office, then return to my original task, pulling open her drawers and fumbling in amongst her office supplies. My hand closes around something, but it's not a key. It's a small, framed photograph. I squint at it, taking in the dated lighting, and recognize the face of a much younger Edward Patterson. My mind goes back to the letter I found in the drawer at Annabelle's. *My child doesn't need to know who their father is and neither does anybody else...*

The child in the photograph is just a baby, dressed all in white and impossible to identify, beyond the stilted smile on

Edward's face. I run a fingertip over the baby, trying to discern any familiarity in their features but the photo is impossible to read. *And where did Louise get it, anyway? Unless...*

I stare at it in shock until I hear footsteps, and I instinctively return the treasure, sliding the drawer closed and straightening just in time for the door to the office to swing open and a figure I recognize to stroll in.

"You aren't Louise." The tall, dark-haired man I've seen several times now but still haven't managed to identify comes to a halt and then tilts his head to one side. "You must be Cassie, right? I've heard a lot about you."

"Oh?" I don't even bother to hide the note of challenge in my voice. "And you are?"

He smiles, and there's something familiar about the crookedness of his lips that almost makes me do a double-take. I can't quite work out how to form my next question when Louise's arrival saves me from trying.

"David! Are you looking for me?" She sails into the office, stopping at the sight of me. "Cassie! I didn't realize you were here too. What perfect timing! I've been wanting to get the two of you together for a meeting ever since...well...for a while now." She's pink-cheeked and cheerful, and I forget the questions I had wanted to ask her. They'll keep. This won't.

"I was hoping to pick up the keys to my room," I say, with a cold look at the stranger who now, at least, has a name. *David.*

"Of course!" Louise reaches into her pocket, pulling out a heavy ring of keys she sorts through before pulling a couple off and handing them to me. "This is for your room, and this is the master for the whole building." Her eyes twinkle with mischief.

"Don't go losing that, now, will you? You know Serenity Suites prides itself on the security of our residents."

I nod primly and fold my hands around the keys, eager to carry on with my tasks but even more eager to find out what David is doing here, and why Louise seems so content to spend time with a man I've been getting a bad feeling about since I first clapped eyes on him. A guy who looks just a bit too familiar...

"Well, David. I suppose you won't mind if I share the news with Cassie, as we're all going to be working together." Louise lays a warm hand on David's arm and I zero in on the familiarity of the gesture. I just have time to arrange my features into something vaguely indifferent before Louise turns back to me. "David is our new partner."

"Silent partner," David puts in, with a wary look.

"Right." Louise beams. "He just promised to invest all the money we need to make Serenity Suites the success I know it can be."

"That's very generous," I allow, wondering just what this slick businessman thinks he can gain from assisting a place like this.

"It's the very least I could do. I know if my father was still here he'd have supported this project. It's only right I carry on his legacy."

"Your father?" I frown, and slowly the pieces sift into place in my mind. The unshakeable familiarity about the man in front of me, his knowledge about the mansion and its belongings. *The photograph in Louise's desk drawer.* "You're Edward Patterson's son."

"I am," David says, reaching forward and offering me his hand, along with a smile that makes him look more like his father than ever. "But don't hold that against me. It's only since his death that I've come to learn very much about him. It's not every day you inherit an empire."

My smile sours. If this is the man who inherited the bulk of Ed Patterson's fortune it means he inherited something else along with it. This is my new landlord. *Or he would be if he wasn't determined to sell my house out from under me.*

<h1 style="text-align:right">Chapter Eleven</h1>

"**D**id you know Ed had a son?"

I'm standing in the center of my soon-to-be new home. I scarcely notice the fact that the rough floor is now soft, springy carpet under my feet and there's a faint fresh-paint smell from the neat magnolia coat on the walls. My mind is completely focused on the person on the other end of my phone, who is, from the noise I can hear in the background, distracted.

"Mindy!"

"Hmm? Oh, Cassie. Sorry." I hear my friend's voice drop as she addresses someone else, and then there's a rustle as she holds the phone away from her mouth. I tap my foot irritably and wait for her to come back. "What were you saying?"

"I was saying," I speak through clenched teeth and force myself to sound calmer than I feel. "That Edward Patterson had a son. Your husband. He had a son. Did you know about this?"

"Of course I knew." Mindy's voice is so light it's almost as if I haven't just given her the kind of news that shatters a person's whole life. "David is a lovely man."

"*David is a lovely man!*" I screech. "Since when have you even known he exists? I certainly didn't."

"Well, he and his father weren't exactly close." Mindy hesitates. "It all happened such a long time ago, before Ed and I got married. He was quite a bit older than me, you know, and it wasn't like he'd been living like a monk all those years. He told me there had been a short-lived romance with a woman who lived several states away now, and that she'd had a child. A son."

I can't quite believe what I'm hearing. It was apparently common knowledge that there existed, somewhere in America, an heir to the Patterson fortune and I had no idea.

"Well, did you know this son is in town?" I ask, feeling certain that I know something my friend doesn't. "He's here, now." I drop my voice to a whisper. "Buying into Serenity Suites."

"Oh, how lovely!"

I blanch, then recover with an irritated sniff.

"Yes. I suppose he needs to reinvest the money he's going to get from selling my street and making a bunch of people homeless."

"You're being dramatic," Mindy says, in the tone of voice I've come to hate. "And you aren't homeless. Where are you right now?"

I look around my future living room and feel a pinprick of irritation. Why is my friend always right?

"That's not important." I sound petulant and take a deep breath before continuing. "What matters is: Ed Patterson had a son and you never bothered to tell me."

"I didn't realize you cared so much." I can hear a note that sounds suspiciously like laughter and am about to point out to my friend that nothing that's happened here in the last few days has been remotely amusing, but before I can say a word, Mindy speaks again. "Cassie? Cassie, I have to go. There's something here I need to deal with. I'll talk to you later, ok? Say hi to David for me."

"Mindy? Wait! Min-" She's dropped the call and I stand with my phone pressed to my ear for a moment in shock before a knock at the door startles me out of my reverie. It comes again and before I have a chance to reply, the door opens and Joe strolls through it.

"Oh, good! You're here." He alters his course and keeps walking straight towards me. "And you aren't busy."

I glance at my phone, then drop it into my purse as I slide it securely onto my shoulder with a weary sigh.

"I guess not. How can I help you, Joe?"

"Actually, I'm the one who's going to help you." He waggles his eyebrows at me and I stare at him as he suddenly grows a little more serious. "I'm going to help you solve a murder."

• • • •

"ALRIGHT, ARE YOU GOING to tell me, or what?"

"Not here."

Joe had decided that his intelligence - that's the word he used *intelligence* like we're a pair of cold-war spies engaged on a mission in enemy territory - is too important to share with me in my room. *The walls have ears, Ms. Clifton*, he'd said, as he led me through the door into my private courtyard. Even that hadn't been private enough for him, and after a moment's consideration he'd kept walking, urging me to keep pace with him until we're standing in the middle of the gardens, empty but for a couple of workmen wrangling a hedge trimmer that whirs noisily in the background.

"Perfect."

I'm assuming that's what Joe says. It's so noisy I can't hear him, but I can be pretty adept at lipreading when I want to be. He says something else, a jumble of words I can't make out, and I regret that my lipreading skills aren't what they used to be.

"What?" I turn to glare at the gardeners. "It's noisy!"

"Exactly." Joe leans closer to me and now I can just about hear his gravelly whisper. "Good cover."

"There are people everywhere!" I say, looking wistfully back towards the building. "At least my room was empty."

Joe shakes his head.

"This is better." He holds my gaze and I see a gleam of excitement in those grey eyes that makes him look younger than I first thought him. He's probably not that much older than me. And I get the feeling he might even have been handsome, once upon a time...

"Cassie!"

His bark makes me jump and I flush, guiltily.

"Sorry." I glance over my shoulder, reassuring myself that the two gardeners are engaged in their work and not watching us. Joe's paranoia is contagious and I lean a little closer until we're only inches apart. "What did you want to tell me about?"

"I've found our killer." He looks so proud of himself that it takes me a minute to latch onto what in his words made me uncomfortable.

"*Our* killer?" I arch an eyebrow.

"Oh, very well. *The* killer." Joe rolls his eyes. "I've been working on a little investigation, and now I think I've got it all sussed out. The trouble is..." He winces. "I don't exactly have any proof. But that's where you come in."

"Me?" My incessant repetition is annoying even me and I shake it off. "What do you mean? I can't help you." *I'm too busy helping the sheriff.*

"What if I told you the killer was right here, under this roof?"

A cold shiver works its way up my spine and I try not to show him how unnerved I feel. I'm not very good at hiding my curiosity for long.

"Who?"

"David Patterson." Joe rolls back on his heels, folding his arms across his front and looking at me expectantly for my reaction. "Ask me why."

"Why?" I parrot, dumbly.

"Money." Joe is nodding now, as if unspooling the mystery here, to me, only makes it clearer to him. "He's Ed Patterson's natural son, ain't he? But when the Ebeneezer Scrooge of Patterson popped his clogs his fortune would automatically go to the wife, unless she's somehow magically taken out of the way." Joe drops his voice to a whisper I can barely hear. "Or *pushed* out of the way."

I suck in a breath. I can see the whole thing now, and my gaze travels past Joe's head to the empty balconies that overlook the garden. My mind overlays them with a memory of the mansion and I picture Jessica arguing with somebody. *You can't be here.* Wasn't that exactly what she'd said to David Patterson when he arrived at the house before the party? I was there, too. I saw that interaction. He was already acting like the house was his and she was just a temporary - and very unwelcome - guest. I can imagine exactly how angry Jessica would have been about him barging into her room in the middle of the party.

"Well?" Joe's still waiting for my reaction and I turn back to look at him, nodding slightly.

"I think you might be right." I hesitate. "But not about the motive. The bulk of Ed's business investments went directly to his son anyway. Jessica only got some ready cash." I frown. "But she was taking her sweet time about vacating the house. I saw them argue about it." I recall the incident at Annabelle's. *Maybe he discovered who was stealing the family heirlooms and decided to challenge Jessica about it!*

Joe smiles.

"Then it looks like we've just solved a murder."

Chapter Twelve

W e decide to go together to report our findings to Sheriff Cooper. Partly, I think, because Joe doesn't want anyone else taking credit for his magnificent powers of deduction. When we arrive at the station, I'm surprised by the easy way he strolls inside, greeting the desk clerk as if he's done it a hundred times before.

"Morning, Ma'am!" He beams at the young girl, who blinks up at him in surprise and smiles. "Wondering if the sheriff is about. Got something I need to speak to him about." I clear my throat and Joe seems to remember, for the first time, that he isn't here of his own volition. "Uh, *we've* got something we want to see him about."

"Hello, Lisa," I say, pushing past my new friend to greet the young desk clerk. The smile she offers me isn't quite as broad as the one Joe got, but I try not to let that rankle too deeply. "It's quite important." I add this to encourage her to move at more than her usual snail's pace, but it isn't all that successful. With the complete lack of urgency only possessed by the young she draws in a long breath and answers me in a slow, lazy drawl.

"Yeah, no. He's here, but he's kind of busy right now." She hesitates and then shoots me a reluctant smile. "You want to leave a message?"

"Fine."

"Well, actually -"

The door swings open just then and Sheriff Cooper steps into the waiting area, clutching an open file he hastily closes and shoves under his arm when he sees us waiting there.

"Detective Price!"

I do a literal double-take before I realize who *Detective Price* is.

"Just Joe now, Sheriff." Joe stands with his hands on his hips and if I didn't know any better I'd assume he was poised to reach for the gun he no longer has strapped around his waist. I frown, wondering why it never occurred to me that Joe had to have had a career before he came to Serenity Suites, and by all accounts it had been a fairly successful one. One, at least, that won him the admiration of Patterson's own humble sheriff's station.

"How can I help you?" Sheriff Cooper asks, before noticing me and offering a weak smile. "Ah, Ms. Clifton. All ok?"

"Not really -" I begin when a familiar voice floats out from the interrogation rooms behind him. I freeze, then look at the sheriff. "Is that Mindy?"

"I can't possibly comment." Bob shoots Lisa a look and she hops up from her seat and scurries off to firmly close the door he left ajar. He holds out his folder as she passes and she obediently takes it from him, leaving him free to focus solely on us.

"If Mindy's here I have a right to know," I tell him, all bluster.

"Why?"

"Well, she's my friend!" I hesitate. "And I can tell you for nothing that she did not do...whatever it is you're accusing her of."

I feel two sets of skeptical eyes fix on me and let out a breath that somehow encourages Joe to step in and change the subject. Which is good, because my mind is racing with a dozen different possibilities for rescuing my friend, and I've completely forgotten the real reason Joe and I came to visit the sheriff today.

"Ms. Clifton and I have been discussing the - uh - the murder at the mansion, Sheriff, and we think we've hit on something rather pertinent to your investigation. Is there someplace we can go and talk?"

"Certainly." Bob glances from Joe to me and back again. "If you can just -" He pauses as Lisa emerges from the back escorting another person I vaguely recognize, although I can't imagine what he's doing here.

"You!" The handsome, sandy-haired man from the bank - and the party - grins at me and makes a mock bow.

"Thank you, Mr. Butler," Bob says, with a weary sigh. "You've been very helpful."

"Glad to be of service," the stranger drawls, glancing at Joe before bowing again and slouching out of the station.

"Do you know that guy?" Joe asks, in a low voice. We have a moment to ourselves while Sheriff Cooper and Lisa exchange a word or two, and I shake my head. It's the truth. I don't know him. But the fact that he's here, at the same time Mindy is here, makes me nervous. Joe's watching me carefully though, and I'm not really surprised at his next words. "You don't have to stay here for this if you have somewhere else you'd rather be."

I frown, then he jerks his head, quick as a flash, after the guy who just left. He stares at me, widening his eyes just a fraction, and then I realize he's trying to tell me something.

"Actually, I do have something important to do. Sheriff, Joe can explain things to you. I have to run!"

I try not to be offended at the momentary flicker of relief that crosses the sheriff's face and trust Joe to pass on what we've worked out about David Patterson, then I bolt through the door and out onto the street, looking one way and then another to try and figure out which way the mysterious stranger went. He's sneakier than I gave him credit for, though, and faster. I've lost him before I've even made it halfway down the street. Coming to a stop, I weigh my options. I could go back to the sheriff's station and rejoin Joe, but I could tell from their blossoming bromance that I'll more than likely be in the way. That rankles but I try not to let it. Instead, I decide to go to the cafe and see if anyone there knows what's happened with Mindy. Somebody is bound to know something, and when I push the door open and slip inside I see Samuel Greenwood manning the coffee machine with a look of desperation on his face.

"Cassie! Oh, thank heavens. Do you know how to work this thing?"

I can help him figure it out. My favorite niece runs a cafe not unlike this one, and having made myself useful there the last time I visited I decide it's not too late to brush up on my skills. Together we manage to make up several not too shabby coffees for the regulars, who don't quite turn their noses up at them, and in a moment's lull I turn to Samuel to ask him what I really want to ask him.

"What happened to Mindy?"

Samuel winces, eyeing the floor, and I can tell he doesn't want to gossip, which is a rarity. Usually, he's at the forefront of Patterson news, and I wonder if it's because Mindy is the subject that he's being reticent.

"I heard she's being interviewed by the sheriff."

"Deputy Davis asked her to go to the station," Samuel says, in a low voice. "Something about items going missing from the mansion."

"Then it's not to do with the murder?" I'm relieved in a way I can't explain, but then I remember that fancy new watch she was wearing. "Hold on, missing items?"

"There have been all sorts of things going missing from the mansion for weeks now. I guess they were already looking into it before Jessica...before what happened. Why they think Mindy had anything to do with it -"

"She didn't!"

"Hey, you don't need to convince me!" Samuel says, taking a step back. "But I think it's going to take more than your say-so to persuade Sheriff Cooper. If Mindy didn't take these things, who did?"

I'm reminded of the angry confrontation between David Patterson and Annabelle at her store. Is there any scandal in Patterson he doesn't have a hand in?

• • • •

WHEN I BURST BACK INTO the sheriff's station I don't necessarily expect a warm welcome but I do expect an acknowledgment. Instead, I see the top of Lisa's head, bent over her phone. At first I think perhaps she hasn't heard me come in, despite the way the door beeps when you open it. I take a step forward and clear my throat.

"One second..." Lisa still doesn't move, and I'm about to bypass her altogether but she must sense it because, with a heroic sigh, she closes whatever app it is that has her so engrossed and looks up. "Yeah?"

Yes. I bite my tongue before offering the corrective, feeling every one of my seventy-plus years, and smile.

"Hello again, Lisa, dear. I just wanted to have a word with Sheriff Cooper. He's back this way, is he? With Joe - with Mr. Price?"

I'm moving as I talk, skirting the reception desk and aiming for the interrogation rooms. I only mean to look for the sheriff, exactly as I say, but Lisa has the suspicions of a terrier and dashes around the side of her desk to intercept me.

"The sheriff's in the middle of an interview, Ms. Clifton. You're more than welcome to wait here."

"Perhaps Deputy Davis then," I babble, knowing full well he's probably still interrogating poor Min about the thefts she certainly isn't responsible for. "Or -"

"Ms. Clifton. Back already?" I can hear the weariness in Sheriff Cooper's voice and it's not until I turn to look at him that I see a twinkle in his eyes that suggests he's not entirely disappointed to see me.

"I was just looking for you! Lisa said you were busy."

"And she'd be right." Bob consults his watch. "But not too busy to spare a moment or two for the Grand Dame of Patterson. Why don't you come through?"

"Where's Joe?" I blurt out, as he leads me into an empty interrogation room. *And where's Mindy?* I couldn't have been the only one to notice that the doors to the other interrogation rooms, far from being locked, stood ajar. Empty, every one.

"I expect he's scouring the town trying to find you!" Bob points me to a chair and settles into the one opposite me. "Now, what was it you wanted to talk to me about?"

"Mindy." I sit, folding my arms and glaring at him. "You know she has nothing to do with this murder business."

"Do I?"

I admire Sheriff Cooper and as far as I'm aware he's very good at his job. But he can also be infuriating at times.

"She's not a murderer," I say, sternly. "And she's not a thief, either."

This is enough to make the sheriff shift in his seat and I can tell I've landed on the real reason he was interrogating her.

"I don't know who tried to tell you she was. It's ridiculous. Why would she steal from a house that used to belong to her?" Bob opens his mouth to reply but I cut him off before he can say a word. "And anyway, those thefts have been going on for weeks. Mindy hasn't been to the mansion since she used to live there. She was only there at the party because she was catering."

"Yes, that's what she says."

"Because it's true!"

"I'm surprised she wanted to cater for a party thrown by her ex-husband's widow." Bob raises his eyebrows. "They weren't exactly close, Mindy and Jessica, were they?"

"That doesn't mean she killed her! If you're going to accuse everyone who didn't like Jessica Patterson of murdering her you're going to end up accusing half the town."

A dark shadow crosses the sheriff's face and the way he looks at me changes almost imperceptibly.

"And half of those people were at the party," I say, with a little less feeling. "With far more opportunity than Mindy, who was busy in the kitchen all night."

"All night?" Bob asks this question quietly, but it lands and I can't fight the blush I feel creeping into my cheeks. "Ms. Clifton?"

"I'm sure she took her breaks just like anybody else. There was only one time I went to look for her in the kitchen and couldn't find her." I pause for less than a breath. "But that was when everyone was clearing up. She was probably rounding up plates from another room."

"And what time was that?"

"I don't recall." I fidget in my chair, feeling inexplicably guilty. I'd gone to look for Mindy just a few minutes before I took my solo walk outdoors and that was just a few minutes before Jessica... But that couldn't mean anything, could it? *Mindy isn't a murderer*, I say to myself, wondering why I need to hear the words again. *She's my friend.*

"Well, Ms. Clifton, you'll be pleased to hear you aren't the only one who struggled to find Mindy at some point during the party. Several of her catering staff suggest that she did indeed take a break - as was her right because it was a long shift she was working." He smiles, grimly. "And no, I don't think the fact that she needed five minutes to herself after catering a whole party makes her a murderer." He draws a breath. "It does mean she had an opportunity to explore the property, though."

"Just like everybody else did! I mean, even me and Louise -"

"Even you and Louise what?"

I bite my lip, frustrated with the fact I keep talking myself in circles and likely dragging more people into the sheriff's orbit of potential killers and sneak thieves.

"We went to speak to Jessica a little while before she died." I lift my head. "Before she died. She was perfectly fine when we left her in her room. Alone."

"Noted." Bob makes an elaborate squiggle on a sheet of paper. "And what did you talk to her about?"

"Oh, nothing very important." *Money. The investment she was supposed to be making into Serenity Suites from the fortune she inherited from her husband...*

"Why are you still looking at different suspects?" I ask, abruptly changing the subject. "Didn't Joe tell you what we've discovered? David Patterson was at the party too and I certainly didn't have eyes on him all evening." I pause. "And he had much more to gain from Jessica's death -"

"You'd think so, wouldn't you?" Bob leans forward, resting an elbow on the table and looking at me. "But it turns out that apart from a small bequest the bulk of Mr. Patterson's estate on his death passed to his son. Apart from no longer having to deal with his stepmother, David wouldn't gain a thing from the death of Jessica Patterson."

"Nor would Mindy!" I put in, eager to defend my friend and make up for disproving her alibi.

"She might if Jessica caught her in the middle of committing a crime. Say, a theft."

"What theft?" I scoff, feeling increasingly anxious about the fate of my friend. With a sigh, Bob flips a few pages in his folder until he comes across a Polaroid photograph. He slides it across the table towards me.

"Have you ever seen your friend wearing this?"

My throat constricts. The photograph is of an elegant, antique rose gold watch. I lift my gaze to meet the sheriff's but say nothing. I don't need to.

"You see, Ms. Clifton? Often we don't know our friends as well as we think we do."

Chapter Thirteen

My head is spinning when I escape the sheriff's station and I drift back towards the cafe, but a peep in the window shows no sign of Mindy. I'm not sure whether to be glad about that or not. I can't help but think back over everything my friend has said to me during our long acquaintance. I know she was angry about the way her marriage ended, and bitter that Jessica Patterson replaced her as the new owner of the mansion but theft? I didn't think her capable of it. Much less murder.

But perhaps I didn't know her very well after all...

My feet steer me along as if of their own accord, and I trace the familiar route back towards my house - or my former house, as I'm going to have to start thinking of it soon.

"Cassie! Oh, Ms. Clifton, did you get your mail yet?"

Tina Lombard is in her front garden again, but her children are nowhere to be seen, and I'm about to remark on it when I register the piece of paper she's clutching in one hand.

"Isn't it the most wonderful news?"

"Hmm?" I lean closer, trying to see what she's holding but she waves it just out of view, leaving me as confused as ever.

"It's not a lot, of course, but it'll be enough to get us and the kids settled somewhere new. We're thinking of moving a couple of towns away so I can be nearer my family. It'll be less of a commute for George, too. A win all round!"

"That's nice dear." I smile blandly, thinking that it doesn't matter what exactly Tina is talking about. If she's happy, I'm happy. And she certainly seems happy. Without warning she throws her arms around me and squeezes me tight.

"Can you believe Mr. Patterson gave us all a lump sum payment for the inconvenience all this has caused? When he's only doing what he wants to do with his own property! They gave us proper notice. It's not like he owed us anything." She laughs. "Not that I'm complaining. A cash injection is certainly a very welcome thing."

"A what?"

Tina's smile falters, and when she speaks again her voice is small.

"Oh, didn't you get your cheque yet?" She tugs on a loose curl, looking unmistakably like her eldest daughter. "Ours arrived in the mail this morning."

I wrangle control of my face once more and give her a reassuring pat on the arm.

"I'm sure mine will be there waiting for me on the mat. I've had a busy day!" It looks like she's about to ask me what I've been up to and I pat her once more on the arm and make my goodbyes. "Now just be sure and give me your new address if you're going to be moving out of Patterson. You needn't think that's enough to escape our friendship!" I smile. "It'll be nice to have someone new to write to." She colors, then gives me another hug, only letting go when one of her children starts up wailing inside the house.

Fumbling with the lock on my front door, my eyes are on the welcome mat as I stumble inside, and there, just as I said there might be, is a stack of mail. I scoop it up, taking care to examine each envelope before selecting the one that looks most likely. I tear it open, smoothing out the letter it contains and just catch a loose cheque as it flutters to the ground. My eyes widen when I see the figure marked *to pay*. And my thumb slides gratefully over the signature *David Patterson*. This is generous. More than generous! I do a quick calculation of the number of people on my street who will have been greeted with this today and think he'll have bought himself no end of good feeling amongst my neighbors. Strangely, it doesn't feel like a publicity stunt. I read the letter, forcing my eyes to focus on it even though they keep straying to my cheque as if I'm afraid it will vanish just as suddenly as it arrived.

"He writes a good letter," I mutter to myself, as I'm forced to offer a grudging admiration of the man who made me homeless. *But not destitute.* I look back at the cheque, thinking that even if this outlay hasn't likely made a dent in his overall financial picture it was still a kind gesture. *And to think, I was all ready to accuse him of murder just a few hours ago!* I straighten, determined to put things right. I need to catch up with Joe again, too, and make it clear to him that however perfect our original solution seemed, it's wrong. *If David Patterson has enough of a fortune he can afford to give it away - long before Jessica's estate is even settled - then he had no financial motive for murder.* I think back to the antagonistic meeting I witnessed but shake my head. *Just because two people don't get on is no reason for them to want each other dead.* And in any case, it seemed like Jessica was the one with the real grudge against him. He'd been indifferent. Amused, even. I read over the letter once more then fold it up, dropping it on the counter with the rest of my mail. The cheque I slide carefully into my purse, then glance around the room. With a sigh, I scoop up another box laden with donations and head out. *If I'm going to the bank I might as well kill two birds with one stone and drop off some donations too!* I check my phone, but there are no missed calls or messages or anything. Irritation pricks at me. Joe has just abandoned me. For all he knows I'm still chasing down what he now knows is a dead lead. *Well, I'll do my jobs and then I'll go and find him and tell him what I think of his temporary "teamwork".* I shoulder my purse, then shift my box into a slightly easier position before striding back down the street for the third time that day.

• • • •

WHEN I REACH ANNABELLE'S store I hesitate for half a moment, performing a peculiar sort of dance in the doorway while I try and free a hand to turn the handle, until another customer beats me to it.

"Let me."

The woman's voice is almost gruff, and when I turn to thank her, her head is down. I continue, anyway. *There's no cost to good manners!*

"Thank you." I cross the threshold quickly, shuffling my grip on my box of donations before dropping it with a dusty thud by my feet. I can kick it along the floor much more easily than I can carry it and last time I checked there's nothing in there very breakable. I glance across at my neighbor and feel a peculiar glimmer of deja vu. "Is it your drop-off day too?" I nod at the bulging tote bag she has slung over one arm, and she turns, swinging it out of view.

"Huh?"

"You were in here earlier, weren't you?" I tilt my head, recognizing her at last. "And hey, I know you. Don't you work for Jessica Patterson?"

"What?" The woman bristles. "I don't know what you're talking about." She takes a step back from me as if she thinks I'm going to lunge at her and I smile, awkwardly. *Since when has five-foot-nothing, grey-haired little old me been intimidating?*

The door swings open again behind me and I turn to see Sheriff Cooper stroll in, his blank expression shifting into a smile when he spots me.

"Ms. Clifton. A pleasure to see you again." He dips his head in that vague allusion to a bow that always puts me in mind of Clark Gable and I smile back, hoping he can't see the blush I can feel creeping over my cheeks as I remember our last meeting. I was so adamant that David Patterson was our killer and now here I am with a cheque he gave me - purely out of his own good-natured generosity - ready to pay in at the bank.

I jump to attention, eager to finish my jobs, and notice that my neighbor has disappeared further into the shop. I dismiss our interaction and focus instead on kick-shuffling my box towards the counter, where I can see Annabelle standing, her attention consumed by a ratty old paperback she's reading from the top of a stack of donations.

"Allow me." Sheriff Cooper scoots around in front of me and lifts the box with effort. "What have you got in here?" He laughs. "Rocks?"

"Try ten years of accumulated memories. I'm relocating." Bob's eyebrows lift. He hasn't heard about my plans for the future. "I'm moving into Serenity Suites."

If it's possible Bob's eyebrows lift even higher, then he seems to recall himself and noisily clears his throat.

"Well, I'm sure you'll be very happy there." He hesitates. "Ma'am."

Ma'am! It's one thing to be Ma'am-ed by a junior deputy young enough to be my grandson, but I'm sure I only have a decade on the man in front of me. *If that!*

"I'm going to work there," I say, archly. "You are looking at the new lifestyle manager." I draw myself up to my full height and resist the urge to make jazz hands. "With my own apartment on site, as a perk of the job. Which works out very well for me, now that my whole street is set to be demolished."

"Well, that's wonderful!" Bob beams, and then his smile drops as he processes the last part of what I've just said. "I mean, about your new home. And your new job! Not the demolition." He drops my box of donations heavily on Annabelle's desk, making her jump, and scattering her pile of paperbacks to the ground.

"Oh, pardon me!" The sheriff drops to a squat and begins retrieving the books, leaving Annabelle to meet my gaze over the chaos with a resigned look.

"Sorry to bring in another box for you already. I'm just trying to keep things moving while I'm motivated." I cheerfully open the box and start pointing out various items and whether I think they'll be profitable to sell.

"And they're all...ah...yours?" Annabelle eyes the sheriff, who stands and passes her an armful of books. "I have to ask now, you see, after...after..."

"We're making some progress on that front," Sheriff Cooper says, then hooks his thumbs through his belt loops.

"Matter of fact, that's why I was coming here to talk to you. I wondered if you'd recovered any more items of - ah - questionable provenance."

Huh?

"No, only the few that Mr. Patterson queried. Although I have had some interesting donations recently." Annabelle moves away from the counter and then beckons the sheriff to follow. I've got no business coming along, but I also don't see either of them telling me not to, and with an air of vague disinterest I keep pace. "I've put a few things to one side -"

"Oh!"

Both Annabelle and Sheriff Cooper turn to look at me, but my attention is fixed on one particular item in the box.

"What is it, Cassie?" she asks. "You see something you want to buy?" I can sense dollar signs flashing in her brain and on any other day I'd have teased her mercilessly about it but right now all I can focus on is the item she grazes with the pinkie finger of her left hand.

"I see something I recognize," I say, reaching for the offending item and wiggling it free of its neighbors. "I don't know about the other items David was upset about the other day, but this one certainly doesn't belong here. It belonged to the elder Mr. Patterson." I glance at Bob. "And Mindy, when they were married."

Both of my companions are surveying me with curiosity now.

"I know because I gave it to them."

Chapter Fourteen

"Are you sure it wasn't just donated? Maybe Mindy -"

I shake my head at Annabelle before she can finish that thought. The last thing I want to do is connect my friend Mindy with more things missing from her former home.

"If Mindy had wanted this she would have taken it when she and Ed first divorced. I'm sure it was just tucked away in a corner somewhere." I turn the paperweight over in my hand. "I don't know why anyone would steal it, but I'm quite sure it wasn't donated. Unless Jessica brought a box of her own things in?"

I glance at Sheriff Cooper, who is wearing a thoughtful sort of frown as he surveys the rest of the things Annabelle has put to one side.

"Can you remember who donated these?"

Annabelle shakes her head.

"But it must have been recent," I put in. "Who all has been in here donating since - since Jessica died?"

"Well, you." Annabelle counts through potential suspects on her fingers and I try not to bristle at the fact that she named me first. Or that her doing so makes the sheriff rock back on his heels and look at me in a way that might have been threatening, if I had any reason to be a suspect.

"Other than me," I grind out, glancing over my shoulder for the other woman who was in the store just five minutes ago. I know she's been in here before. A slow prickle of recognition tugs at me and I lay a hand on Jessica's arm, making her flinch. "Who was that woman, the one who was here when I was here?" I turn to Sheriff Cooper. "You saw her, right? Blonde, frizzy hair. I'm sure she was at the mansion."

"At the party? That's half the town."

"No, before that." I bite my lip. "She was hovering around Jessica when they were getting ready for the party earlier in the day. Like an assistant of some kind."

"Assistant!" Annabelle laughs, self-deprecatingly. "Maybe if I had one of those I'd be able to remember who donated what around here."

She doesn't seem to realize - or care - just how important this revelation might be, but I think Bob does, or at least he sees I'm upset. When a glance around the interior of the store confirms our mystery woman isn't there, he frowns.

"I need to get back to the station." He eyes me, and I'm worried he's about to ask me to accompany him. *Then again, if it's between me and Mindy...*

"Shall I come with you?"

The question is out before I can stop myself, and I earn a look of surprise from the sheriff and one of suspicion from Annabelle.

"Is there anything else you have to share, Ms. Clifton?" Bob all but winks at me and I recall his unofficial request for me to keep my ear to the ground on all things murder-y. I guess that includes all things theft-y, now, too. I shake my head, and to my surprise, he pats me awkwardly on the arm. "Not to worry then. I'll be sure to reach out if I need your help again. Don't forget, I know where you live." He smiles, and I realize he's teasing me.

"Was there anything else *I* could help you with?" Annabelle has little interest in my living arrangements, or Sheriff Cooper's investigations, as long as they don't implicate her or her shop, and she bustles back to work. I feel a stinging reminder of the cheque I've yet to pay into the bank and decide I'll get my jobs done as quickly as I can before heading to Serenity Suites. My head is reeling and I could do with a sit down and a chat with a friendly face. Louise is sure to listen to me and sympathize on how best to deal with the Mindy problem. Surely now, at least, Sheriff Cooper will be looking for someone else as a potential thief. *And a potential murderer.* I shiver and hurry out of the store and down the street towards the bank.

· · · ·

TRACEY IS ONCE MORE manning the desk as I make my way into the bank, although it takes me several moments to catch her attention. Her gaze is fixed on the window of her boss's office and even though his door is closed even I can detect raised voices.

"Problem?" I ask, fishing in my purse for the cheque I want to fill in.

"Not at all!" Tracey's smile doesn't reach her eyes, and she seems to wilt as she looks at me. "Well, possibly. That man." She nods towards the office, wincing at one particularly loud, muffled shout. "Made Jane cry." She drops her voice to a whisper, and I lean forward to listen, despite myself. "He came in demanding access to a safety deposit box and we couldn't give it to him. It was embargoed, you see, and when the police are involved like that there's nothing we can do. He didn't seem to understand. It wasn't about us not being helpful, it's about breaking the law, and that's just not the sort of place this branch of the Stellar National Bank is." She pauses and I make an encouraging noise as I continue to rummage in my bag. I have a firm hold on my cheque, but I feel like as soon as I hand it over, Tracey will get distracted with work and I'll lose my opportunity to find out what's going on. *Gossip*, I tell myself, then remember that I still just about have police authority to keep my ear to the ground. *This could be a clue*, I think, determined to store every detail in my brain for later reflection.

"Did you catch his name?" I ask, risking a glance over my shoulder. The man, whoever he is, has his back to me, and through frosted glass, it's impossible to make out his features anyway. But he seems shorter than the other stranger to Patterson I half thought it might be. My spirits lift, and I emerge with my cheque pinched between my thumb and forefinger. I've just about come around to liking David Patterson, so I don't want to think of him making poor bank tellers cry.

"Who?" Tracey is looking past me again, her piercing gaze trying to see to the very center of the drama unfolding in her boss's office. "Oh." She shakes her head. "No, but the funny thing was the safety deposit box he wanted to access..." She pauses as if thinking better of sharing a confidence. My skin prickles with excitement. I feel like this is it, the clue I hoped to find. I start talking before I've even really decided what to say.

"Don't tell me he was trying to access someone else's security deposit box? I've heard about scams like this. My niece, Meredith..."

"Oh, no! It wasn't that. At least, not entirely." Tracey frowns. "The safety deposit box was in his name, but he wasn't the only beneficiary. He shared access with..." She trails off, looking very uncomfortable and I arrange my features in a smile I hope is encouraging, rather than eager.

"With who, dear? I thought these sorts of things were limited to spouses." I hesitate. "I expect they've had a little falling out, have they, him and his wife?"

Tracey bites her lip, glancing around to reassure herself there's no way we can be overheard.

"The other signatory on the box wasn't his wife. It was Jessica Patterson!"

I reel back at this information, but before I have time to react the door to the office bangs open, and the man inside storms out.

"This is completely unreasonable. It's my safety deposit box. I should be allowed access to it whenever I want!"

"Sir, please. Mr. Butler...!"

I turn and freeze in place. I *do* recognize this man after all. He isn't David Patterson, but there's no mistaking the handsome face of the other stranger I've noticed milling around town lately. He catches me looking, and instead of smiling, scowls.

"What are you staring at, Grandma?"

Grandma? I'm about to give him a piece of my mind about respecting one's elders, but Sheriff Cooper beats me to it. I'm not entirely sure when he stepped into the bank - perhaps the staff called him to deal with this particularly unruly customer - but his timing, on this occasion, is impeccable.

"What seems to be the problem?"

"The problem, *Sheriff*, is that this bank is holding certain items of mine and refusing me access to them. That's illegal, isn't it?" The man's voice drips with sarcasm, and I see an almost imperceptible shift in Sheriff Cooper's stance. I swallow my irritation with the man and hold my ground, ready to watch the fireworks. Any chance this stranger had of winning the sheriff over to his side is gone, and he's about to feel the full force of the law around here.

"Is that so?" He speaks slowly and quietly, in a tone of voice that most people might mistake for stupid, but those of us who've lived in Patterson more than a hot minute know is dangerous.

"I just want my things!" The stranger is seething now, speaking through clenched teeth as if to an army of simpletons. "You have no right to keep them from me!"

"The deposit box is registered under two names, sir, and without permission from both owners, I cannot surrender its contents. I explained that to you."

"Well, what good is that?" The stranger whirls around to glare at the bank manager, who is white-faced and shaking from the stress of this encounter. "When the other owner is dead?!"

Chapter Fifteen

"**T**hen what happened?!"

I'm sitting with Louise in the shell of Serenity Suites' soon-to-be cafe, sipping instant coffee from a paper cup and trying to imagine what this place will look like when it's finished. It's so close now I can almost see it, and with a final coat of paint and some new furniture, I can imagine it being somewhere I will spend a lot of time.

"Cassie!"

I whip my head around and look guiltily at my friend. I'd been telling her about my day, all the complicated mess of it, and left off at the most important part.

"Well, that's the crazy thing. This stranger - Mr. Butler - is Mr. *Carl Butler*, of Oakland Ridge." I pause and when Louise still hasn't made the connection, add the context I know she's missing. "The same Oakland Ridge that Jessica Patterson – formerly Butler - is from."

"They're related?" Louise wrinkles her nose. "I didn't know Jessica had a brother."

"She didn't." I take a sip, waiting for the penny to drop. When Louise is still frowning in confusion after a moment I realize I'm going to have to explain that, too. "He's her husband." I hesitate. *Widower?*

"No." Louise shakes her head. "No, she was married to Ed Patterson. So this Carl Butler is her ex-husband?" She raises her eyebrows. "What's he doing in Patterson? Horrible timing...or is that why he's back?"

I take another sip of my lukewarm coffee, grimace, and swallow.

"He was her ex-husband, technically." I pause. "But not legally." I don't need to look at Louise this time to sense the shock register on her face.

"Then that means…"

"That's right." I nod slowly. "Jessica Butler was never legally married to Ed Patterson. Any money she would have inherited from him goes straight back into his estate."

"Right." Louise's foot is jiggling nervously from side to side. "What is he doing here, then? This real husband? He knows she's dead, right?"

I'm a little surprised by the matter-of-fact tone of voice, but when I glance at my friend, her features are pinched and pained, as if she's struggling to process all I'm telling her.

"He knows now." I finish the rest of my story, explaining Sheriff Cooper's precipitous arrival, and how the outraged Carl Butler ended up betraying himself, his ex-wife, and their third partner in crime, Harriet Darnell.

"Harriet Darnell. Why do I know that name?"

"She was the Pattersons' housekeeper. She's also been gradually smuggling items out of the house to sell or conceal before the whole estate passes into David's hands." I wince. "A little insurance policy for Jessica, it seems."

"Right." Louise lets out a bitter little laugh. "Well, I guess that explains why she was so reluctant to give me the money she promised to invest. She didn't have any!"

"Oh, she did." I drain the last of my coffee and toss my empty cup in the trash. "She'd managed to keep her marriage a secret, and so long as she kept Butler quiet, she would have inherited just as Ed had planned. Not a lot, but enough to keep her very comfortable. Even if she did have to pay a percentage in hush money to keep Carl quiet. That's why he came to town. Her payments dried up."

"So he killed her." Louise's words are quiet, and it's almost like she's piecing together a solution, rather than asking a question. I frown. It's the same thorny issue I've been turning over in my mind all afternoon. Carl Butler would be the perfect solution to the two mysteries that have been plaguing Patterson lately - the thefts from the mansion and the murder of Jessica Patterson - his wife. But what would killing her do for him, other than curtail his monthly payments? It'd lose him access to the house, too, and any property he could sell in the meantime.

"I don't think so," I say, after a long moment of silence. "As he said, she'd have been more likely to kill him. His death would ensure nobody need ever find out about their existing marriage. She could have inherited just as she planned, and sailed away into the sunset, free and clear. The longer he hovered around Patterson, the more he threatened to out her secret, the more fearful she was that she would lose everything."

"Right. I guess it's understandable she wanted a fresh start when she came here. She isn't the first person to change her name." Louise tugs on her locket, that same gold stylized *S* she wears like a talisman. She catches my gaze and pours the last of her coffee down the sink, before tossing it into the trash with mine. "So they still haven't figured out who killed her?" She shrugs. "Maybe it really was just an accident. Too much champagne." She smiles, and I'm a little startled by her apparent good cheer. "Couldn't happen to a nicer person." She turns, catching sight of somebody she greets with a wave. "Joe! I was wondering where you'd got to. How are you settling in?"

"Just fine, Louise, thank you." Joe winks at me. "Cassie."

"Joe." I scowl at him, still waiting for an apology from him for ditching me earlier that day. My irritation only serves to amuse him, though, and I figure if I want an apology I'll be waiting a long time. "Did you enjoy your visit to Patterson?"

"It was certainly interesting to explore the place a bit." He grins, flicking his attention back to Louise. "Cassie was kind enough to show me around the town. Introduce me to a few people. Your sheriff is a great guy. Just the kind of person I used to look forward to dealing with, back in the day."

"Joe here was some big deal in the police force," I say, to save my friend yet more confusion.

"I was not!" Joe is all affrontery, and I'm pleased that for once I'm the one getting a rise out of him. "I was a detective, I'll have you know."

"Yeah, right. And I was a Rockette."

Joe arches an eyebrow and I blush, cursing myself for letting him so easily turn the tables. *And really. Detective? This guy?*

"Well, I'm glad you're settling in." Louise straightens and begins walking swiftly towards the door. "I'm afraid I'd better dash. Lots to do!"

It could just be because she's walking away from us at speed, but something in Louise's voice sounds jumpy and unsettled, and I wait until she's out of earshot before turning to glare at Joe.

"You didn't have to upset her like that! We were having a serious conversation."

"Oh yeah? What about?" Joe gestures around us. "In case you hadn't noticed, this is a public area." He draws a line with the toe of one faded boot in the dust. "And not exactly a finished one, either."

"That's what you get for moving in early," I counter with a glare that fades when I recall I ought to remain professional with the residents here, even if that resident is particularly adept at getting under my skin. "What happened to you earlier, anyway? I went to the sheriff's station to look for you and you disappeared."

"Sorry." Joe's grin suggests he is emphatically *not* sorry. "I was having a look around. Getting a feel for the place. Following a lead."

I roll my eyes. *Following a lead.* Only one of us was actively trying to figure out the truth today, and it certainly wasn't Joe. I turn to walk away but something pins me in place and with a reluctant sigh I turn back.

"What lead?"

"Aha! I thought you might be interested. Come with me, and I'll show you." He makes a performative bow and offers me his arm in an old-school display of chivalry.

• • • •

"WHERE ARE WE?" I ASK as he leads me down a maze of corridors, upstairs, and through another precarious arena of power tools, paint-pots, and half-finished walls.

"What kind of a lifestyle manager can't recognize the third floor of her own building?"

"The kind that's never been up here before," I mutter, narrowly avoiding tripping over a chainsaw left dangerously unattended in the middle of the floor. "Should we even be here?"

Joe shrugs.

"Nobody stopping us, are they?"

That was true, but it's obvious to me that this part of the building isn't exactly finished and open for inspection, either. I clamp down my objections and follow, eager to discover what had him so energized downstairs.

"Here." He opens one of several identical doors and ushers me into a room that looks a lot more finished than the rest of the corridor. "They've been making the rooms nice first and foremost. Want something to show off to prospective buyers, don't they?" He winks, and I admire the elegant furniture arrangement that makes this particular room look warm and inviting.

"Maybe I should move in here," I murmur, thinking of the work I still need to do to my downstairs apartment and wondering how long it'll be before that place feels like home.

"Sure, hide away from all of us in your very own ivory tower." Joe teases. "Not a very for-the-people attitude, is it?"

"I was only joking," I say, flopping down on a surprisingly comfortable wicker chair. "Now what did you bring me here to look at? It's a very pretty room, but as you say, it's all for show. What's the point?"

"Not in here." Joe keeps walking, pulling apart two long, flowing curtains that obscure a pair of doors opening out onto a balcony. I feel a sudden flash of memory and jump up from my chair, following him outside.

"It's you! You were up here! When I was in the garden and I saw a shadow..."

"Yeah." Joe has the grace to look a little guilty. "Guess I scared you, huh? I didn't mean to. I just wanted to check a few things out."

"Like?" I turn away from the garden, fold my eyes, and glare at him.

"Like how someone could successfully push a person over the edge of a balcony without stepping out onto it themselves." Joe puts himself between me and the railings of the balcony. "Imagine I'm the victim, right?"

"Jessica," I remind him, feeling the hairs start to rise on the back of my neck. There's something creepy about reenacting a murder, especially one I witnessed from several feet below. I peer over Joe's shoulder and imagine what Jessica's last view would have been with a shudder.

"Jessica. Right." Joe doesn't seem to notice my discomfort. He smiles and steers me around a little so I'm facing him directly. "So she's probably a little bit smaller and skinnier than me, I'll bet." He pats his vast midsection and I fight the urge to smile. "But even so, to get her to fall backward over a wall - her balcony had a railing, right?"

I nod.

"Even for someone half my size, that's got to be quite a shove. And you said you didn't see anyone. That means whoever it is must have shoved her from inside the room." He grips me by the shoulders and walks me back into the doorway, before squinting over his shoulder. "I reckon from there you'd be pretty much invisible to someone down below. Shove me."

"What?"

"Shove me."

"I'm not going to push you over a balcony!"

"Ha." Joe rolls his eyes. "I'd like to see you try. That's exactly what I'd like you to do. Come on. Push me."

I shake my head, but he's being so infuriating about wanting to prove his point that I give him a little tap.

"Thanks. That's terrible." He draws himself up to his full height, folding his arms and glaring at me. "Try again."

I shove harder - but not enough to move him more than a half-an-inch or so. A third try is enough to make him take a step back but he's soon regained his equilibrium and moved only a pace or two out onto the balcony.

"That's what I thought," he muses, more to himself than to me. He turns to survey the ground, his features drawn into a frown as if he's considering something. "Whoever pushed her would have to come all the way out onto the balcony to do it. Are you sure you didn't see anything?"

I close my eyes, playing the scene over again in my memory like it's a movie. I pause, rewind, replay it, trying to hold tight to the memory and not let my imagination get in the way. I shake my head.

"There was a shadow, maybe, but I couldn't see anything. It was only when I heard the shout -"

"Heard? What did she say?"

"Jessica?" I shake my head. "She screamed as she barrelled over the edge. And she cried out for someone to help." I shiver, then freeze. *She cried out for someone to help.* My throat constricts and I see black around the edges of my vision. This can't be true. It can't be. And yet...

"Cassie?" Joe's voice is soft, almost gentle, as if he's talking to a child or a wounded animal. I can see now how easy it would be to confide in a man looking at me with the compassion he is now. I want to share what I've realized. I do. He helped me remember it, after all. I open my mouth to begin.

"It's nothing." I snap my mouth closed and smile, but I don't think the expression is very convincing. "Can we go back inside? It's cold out here!"

Joe steps aside and we make our way back into the showroom. He steals a glance at me that betrays he's sensed something is wrong but he doesn't press me and for that I'm grateful.

"How's your moving plans going?" He changes the subject, subtly shifting the mood of our conversation. "You need any help?"

"Are you offering to help?" I'm not surprised when he rolls his eyes.

"I may be retired but I ain't dead yet." He places his hands on his hips. "I can carry a box or two." He hesitates and clears his throat. "If you need it, I mean."

"That's very kind. Thank you. I'll think about it."

We're back out on the corridor and I get the sense he's reluctant to leave this floor, and the investigation. I, for one, can't wait to be back in the busier, more finished part of the building, so I can revisit the niggling memory that's just surfaced. *I can't have heard what I thought I heard. It's my imagination playing a trick on me. It has to be.* But even as I think this, I know there's only one way I can find out for sure.

"Well, I'll say goodbye for now. I'd better go and get on with things."

"Sure." Joe lingers, and I sense his decision to say when he glances at me. "Can you find your way back downstairs ok?"

"I'll be fine. No more balcony acrobatics, ok? At least not without making sure there's a ladder nearby."

He lets out a grim hoot of laughter and waves me away, and as soon as I'm out of his line of sight, I pick up my pace and hurry down the stairs at close to a run. I power-walk down the corridor, barely breathing until I reach Louise's office. The door is closed and I knock, holding my breath until she invites me in.

"Hi, Cassie!" She smiles at me across her desk, looking happier than I've seen her in days. "Isn't it great? It looks like everything is finally coming together at last!"

"It does." I return her smile with one of my own, but evidently, it's much less convincing to Louise than it was to Joe. A shadow settles over her features, and I don't even have to ask the question I'm still struggling to form in my mind.

"You know, don't you?"

Chapter Sixteen

My blood runs cold in my veins and as I feel my knees start to buckle I slide into the seat opposite her, finding it quite ridiculous that I'm sitting across a desk from my friend, colleague, *boss* as if we're discussing more pertinent Serenity Suites details and not a murder.

"How did you figure it out?" Louise tugs on her necklace, that same sparkling letter *S* that I have noticed her playing with more and more lately. "I thought they'd just assume it was an accident...then, of course, with those thefts, it seemed like I'd found the perfect scapegoat. After all, if someone's a thief they're just as likely to be a murderer, right?" She shakes her head, ruefully. "I didn't bank on that person being Mindy though. I didn't mean for her to be implicated. Or anyone." She looks at me, coldly. "And I certainly didn't mean for you to witness the whole thing. If only you hadn't, this might all have turned out ok."

"Simone," I say slowly, testing out the name as if it's the first time I've heard it. It very nearly is. "I thought Jessica had been calling out to *someone* to help her, but she was saying *Simone*. She was calling out to *you* to help her.

Louise scowls.

"She always knew I hated that name. It was her last bit of power to hold over me. My father gave me it, you see. It's all Mom ever told me about him, that he was married and didn't want any involvement with us, but he had given me that name. A family name." Her lips quirk in disgust. "I dropped it just as soon as I could. Louise suits me much better." She looks at me. "Jessica found a letter my mother had written to Edward telling him about...about me. She put two and two together and worked everything out. That's why he took me under his wing, working as his assistant. It's why he was so supportive of my work here. But then she decided to use that knowledge against me, and suggested she'd keep my secret if I let her keep her money." Louise's eyes flash. "*Her money*. Edward promised that donation to me. He didn't have time to write anything formal about it, of course, but we all knew that was what he wanted. What I deserved." Her voice rings with bitterness.

"So you argued?" I still can't quite believe Louise went back to Jessica's room that night to kill her. "After we left, you went back?"

"I tried to reason with her one last time, but she was insistent. She didn't care about me, or my plans. She was taking what was hers and putting Patterson in the rearview." She tosses her head in almost perfect mimicry of Jessica's flirtatious habit. "It didn't seem fair that she could just do that. Walk away, as if none of this ever mattered." Louise's hands tighten on the edge of her desk. "Patterson is all I have. Serenity Suites is everything to me. And she couldn't even spare me the little investment I'd been promised."

"You lashed out at her."

"She was just so smug!" Louise's face transforms into a snarl. "She told me that Patterson was just a pitstop and she was on her way to bigger and better things. Of course I lashed out. I shoved her, but she'd had too much to drink - and she was wearing those ridiculous heels she could barely walk in. She tripped. She fell." Louise's voice drops to almost a whisper. "It wasn't my fault."

"But you could have helped her," I protest. "She called out to you."

"She called out for *Simone*." Louise's expression sets like flint. "And I've lost count of how many times I've told her *Simone* is not my name." She smiles, a cold, menacing sort of smile that makes me shiver. "I guess she finally took that seriously."

"So what now?" I ask, realizing there's no easy way for either of us out of this tiny office. I'm nearer the door than she is, but she's a lot younger and stronger than me and will be on top of me before I can open it. I reach into my purse, fumbling for my phone with one hand while I strain to keep Louise's gaze fixed on mine. "You got the money you needed from David." I try to smile. "Your brother. Does he know you're his sister?"

"Nope, and he doesn't need to!" Louise's features fall at the mention of this. "Edward Patterson was no kind of father to me when he was alive. I don't need his legacy now." She draws a breath. "But I certainly don't mind accepting his money. Thank goodness David is a lot more detail-oriented about things like that. We've already had the contracts drawn up, and the cash should be in my accounts by the end of the week." She swallows. "Which is why I'm so sorry you had to figure all this out now. We could have worked well together, Cassie. Made this place something really special. I guess now I'm going to have to start all over again with finding your replacement…"

I risk a glance down at my phone - typing without seeing the screen has never been my forte - and then the worst possible thing happens. *It starts ringing.* A tinny, vibrating rendition of a cheesy old pop song starts reverberating around the room, making us both jump, but Louise is quick to recover herself.

"Aren't you going to answer that?"

I look away for a moment, just long enough to lift my phone out of my bag and glance at the display, but it's all the time Louise needs. When I lift my head, I see she has a gun pointed directly at me.

• • • •

"A GUN? WHERE ON EARTH did you get a gun from?"

"Stop questioning me."

"But Louise, this is Patterson! Nobody carries guns around here."

"Plenty of people carry guns, Cassie." I can hear the derision in her voice, and it's almost enough to overcome the absurdity of our situation. "Believe me, Patterson isn't all sunshine and rainbows."

"If you say so." I trip on a loose floor tile and pitch forward, but Louise, who is walking right beside me, is quick to pull me upright again. "Thank you."

"You're welcome."

If she recognizes the absurdity of politeness between us at the moment - a confessed murderer and her soon-to-be second victim - there's nothing in her stony expression that suggests it.

"Must we walk so quickly?" I feign breathlessness and slow my pace almost imperceptibly. "We climbed ever so many flights of stairs and I have to admit I'm not quite as young as I used to be."

My frail-older-lady act might have worked on the sheriff and his deputies, but Louise isn't so easily convinced.

"You managed just fine running around here with Joe an hour ago," she points out, drily, and I'm stunned to silence. *Did she know about that?* I feel a cold chill at my neck, wondering just how closely Louise has been watching me without me realizing it. *Mind you, she's been living a double life for years. I guess she's used to hiding in the shadows.*

My phone call hadn't been rescue - as I'd hoped. It had been Joe, who had received my attempt at a text message - a string of senseless gobble-de-gook - and called me, thinking I might be having a stroke. When I reassured him, through gritted teeth, that I was perfectly fine, and planning to stay and do some work around the site with Louise, he'd ended the call, but not before agreeing to run into Patterson on an errand I hastily fabricated. None of this had been my plan, of course, but when your former friend is pointing a gun at you and directing your words, there's not much you can do but comply.

At least Joe will be safe, I think, although I'm not sure how much faith I can put in that. He might be off-site at this moment, but if I don't get out of this mess somehow, it'll only be a matter of time before he crosses Louise in one way or another, and then what? *He's a big boy*, I tell myself. *He'll be just fine.* I gulp, as Louise directs me down the hallway to the very room Joe and I had stepped into. *Me, on the other hand...*

"What are we doing here?" I ask, as Louise shuts and locks the door behind us. She hesitates, then wedges the wicker chair under the door handle, securing us in the small room.

"We're going to have ourselves a little re-enaction," Louise says, as she straightens and re-orients her aim towards me. "That's what you and Joe have been up to, isn't it? Figuring out what happened on the mansion balcony." She looks around the room with a disdainful little smile. "This isn't quite as grand as Jessica's master bedroom, but it'll have to do."

"What do you mean?" My voice squeaks a little and I swallow, trying not to betray how very disconcerting it is to be staring down the barrel of a gun, and faced with the prospect of being pushed off a very high balcony. Neither of these options is how I saw my older years playing out, and I can't believe I was foolish enough to get myself into such a dilemma. "Louise, dear," I clear my throat, trying to re-establish something of a balance between us. "You can't mean...you've known me for years!"

"I knew Jessica a long time too," Louise said, coldly.

"But - but that was just an accident." I smile, hoping my expression offers more reassurance than I feel. "Wasn't it? Just an accident. Come on, dear. Put that gun down, and we'll go together to Sheriff Cooper and explain it all."

For a moment I think it's worked. She seems to believe me. The gun lowers, and for the tiniest instant, I see a glimpse of freedom.

"Now, that's a lovely idea, Cassie." She matches my overly bright tone with one of her own but turns it mocking and cruel in a way that feels almost like a physical blow. "But I don't want my name tied to even an accidental death."

"But - but what about this?" I glance over my shoulder at the doors to the balcony, which are mercifully closed, but I'm being backed towards them against my will and it's only a matter of time before I'm forced to open them.

"This?" Louise cocks her head to one side.

"Surely you don't want a scandal tied to Serenity Suites." I try one last desperate push for reason. "After everything you've been through to get this place off the ground." My mind is racing. "Ophelia Roy certainly won't want to live in a place where there's been a murder!"

It's so absurd it works. Louise laughs and lets down her guard. As soon as her gun drops I strike, swinging my purse violently with one hand and knocking the weapon out of her hands and clear across the room. With a snarl, she dives after it and I'm left with a horrible choice - fight past her to get to the door that will lead me safely back into the building or burst out onto the balcony and trap myself there. I don't have long to make a decision, and acting almost on impulse, I fly through the doors and start to shout.

"Help!" I cry, wondering why today, of all days, seems to be a holiday for all the workmen I'm used to seeing dotted all around the place. There's not a sound of a power tool or the sight of a hi-vis jacket, but I scan the ground for them all the same. "Please!" I cry. "Someone, help me!" I'm reminded of Jessica's words and wonder, desperately, if I'm about to meet the same fate she did. I drop to my knees, determined to stay low to the ground. If Louise wants to push me off this balcony, she's going to have to come right out here in the open to do it. "Help!" I try again. "Somebody!"

"Cassie?"

I almost think I imagine it, but no, there's a familiar voice floating up from several feet below me.

"Joe?" Relief floods my limps and I raise a shaking hand to catch his attention. "You have to help me! It's Louise! She -"

"Cassie?" Louise's voice rings out loudly somewhere above my head, and I feel her hand close around my shoulder, her sharp fingers digging into my collarbone. "Oh, hello, Joe!" She waves to him, keeping a tight grip on me. "Not to worry! Poor

Cassie seems to have had a bit of a funny turn. I'll keep an eye on her!"

Even though I'm hunched down near the ground I can tell from the way the pressure of Louise's hand on my shoulder tightens that Joe accepts her words and has now disappeared out of sight. My heart sinks. That was it, my one chance at freedom, and I blew it.

"Well, I guess now we'll have to go back to my first plan," she murmurs, low enough that her voice won't carry. "I can't risk another witness to an accidental fall from a balcony. Not that this distance would do more than break a leg."

I'm shaken that my friend Louise can talk so casually about death and injury - while she's debating how to do away with someone. With me! Slowly, my shock solidifies into outrage. I'm angry that she thinks she has the right to act like this. Just because Serenity Suites is important doesn't mean she can kill people to keep it going. I shake free of her grip, knocking her away with a ferocity that surprises even me and now we're both standing on much more equal footing. My confidence only lasts a moment, though. As soon as Louise regains her footing, I realize I haven't won anything.

"What now, Cassie?" she asks, her voice a cynical sing-song. "We're both stuck here."

"Not for long," I tell her. I look over the edge of the balcony, spotting something she hasn't, and am momentarily pleased to see her stunned as I climb over the balcony rail all by myself.

"What are you doing? Cassie!"

"Finding another way down," I say. I don't jump - instead, I lean out, closing my eyes and praying as my hand closes on the top rung of a ladder.

Chapter Seventeen

"There we go!"

Joe is standing on the ground, holding the workman's ladder steady while I scurry down it.

"What, I don't even get a thank you? You looked a little panicked up there." He glances up, his features sinking into a frown as he grows serious. "What's going on?"

"It's Louise," I say, my knees buckling slightly as I find my feet on safe, solid ground again. I fumble for my phone with shaking hands and in the end, thrust it at Joe. "Call the sheriff. Louise's the one. She killed Jessica. And she tried to kill me."

"What?" Joe's too busy looking at me to make the call, and in the end, I force myself to do it. "You can't just leave her in there. She might get away!"

"I can't go back in there," I say, continuing to walk away from the building. "She has - she *had* - a gun."

Joe lets out a low whistle, and I see him turn his head as if debating a solo takedown of our murder suspect.

"Hold on," he says. "I have an idea."

He sprints off - as much as a man of his age and gait can ever sprint - leaving me alone while I wait for Lisa to connect my call to Sherrif Cooper. Fortunately, he seems to hear from the breathless, anxious pitch of my voice that something's badly wrong, and he promises me he's already on his way. I hear the slam of a car door in the background before we end our call and let out a shaky breath before sinking down on the grass to wait for him to come.

Louise is the one. I hear my words repeating in my brain. *Louise killed Jessica. Louise...Simone...Someone.* I can't believe my friend who I trusted, who gave me a job and a home just tried to kill me. She might, even now, be bringing Joe's long and storied life to a sudden close. I look around, wishing he hadn't left me, but then I see him strolling back as if he hadn't a care in the world. He's even smiling!

"What happened?" I ask, unsure if I want to know. He tosses something towards me and I flinch until I see a screwdriver hit the grass in front of me. Wincing, Joe lowers himself gingerly to the ground, groaning a little as his old joints crack in protest. Mine are still so flooded with adrenaline I don't feel a thing, but I already know it's going to be a struggle to get up again.

"Just made sure our perp couldn't get away." He grins. "First I moved the ladder. Can't have her copying your rescue, after all."

"My hero," I say, with an ironic smile.

"Then I barricaded the door down from the top floor. Like you said, it's still a building site up there, so I had plenty of things to hand. She might be able to get out of that room, but she won't be able to get down. Not unless she fancies a long drop."

We both hear the faint sound of sirens and I let out a breath I wasn't aware I'd been holding.

"You did good work, Cassie," he said. "Although you shouldn't have confronted her on your own." He looks stern for a minute. "That's a rookie mistake."

"I see." I pluck at a few blades of grass, hoping the shaking in my hands will stop soon. "So what's your long-honed detective advice for next time I have a criminal cornered?"

"Wait for your partner to come and back you up." He offers me his hand, and after a moment's hesitation, I take it. *Partner.* I couldn't have figured out what Louise had done - or who she really was - without Joe's help. I would still be trapped on the balcony with her without his ingenuity. *I guess maybe we do work well together after all.*

• • • •

"CASSIE! CASSIE, ARE you alright?"

Serenity Suites has never been so busy. Ever since Sheriff Cooper arrived to arrest Louise, there has been a steady stream of people *just stopping by* both me and Deputy Davis are struggling to keep them at bay.

"Min!" I hug my friend, surprised when she isn't the first to let go. At last, she does release me, and that's when I see the deep worry lines etched into her familiar face.

"I couldn't believe it when I heard! And then I just came over here straight away to make sure - because...because..."

"I'm fine," I say, feeling even more confident that that's the truth, now that I've had to reassure so many other people of my wellbeing. It's actually been kind of nice, to know so many people care. I could have coped without the near-death experience to prove that, though.

"Ah, Ms. Clifton...!"

I catch Deputy Davis's eyes. Mindy and I have strayed too close to the Serenity Suites building, which is still a crime scene and closed to visitors. Taking my friend by the arm, I steer her around to the tree-lined parking lot and we sit on the solitary bench to catch up properly.

"Did you know about Louise?"

"I still can't believe it." Mindy shakes her head. "That she killed Jessica. I mean, we both know there was no love lost between me and that woman, but to think of - of killing her!"

"I don't think Louise truly meant to do it." I shiver, recalling the uncanny way my friend's familiar features transformed when she threatened me. Jessica's death might have been partly an accident, but mine certainly wouldn't have been. "I guess we'll never really know what was going on inside her head," I say, wishing the words offered any amount of comfort. "But she'll be locked away now, and hopefully getting the help she needs."

"So what happens to this place?" Mindy's gaze sweeps the parking lot and comes to rest on the building. "It was so close to being finished."

"That's all Louise wanted, I think. To make her dream a success. It just took over. And now..." I swallow. The idea of Serenity Suites thriving - of Louise somehow winning after everything that happens feels wrong. But so, too, does the thought of closing down when we were so close to opening. *It wasn't a bad dream, just because Louise chose the wrong way to pursue it.* "I suppose a lot will depend on our investors," I say, vaguely. "And whether anyone else wants to step up and run the place."

"What about you?" Mindy nudges me sharply in the side. "You were going to be living and working there, anyway. Why not carry on and do exactly as you planned?" Her features drop. "Or can't you bear the thought of being there now?" She sighs.

"I thought that was how I'd feel seeing inside the mansion again, but you know, it wasn't like that at all." She toys with her cuff and I notice she's still wearing the rose-gold watch.

"I thought you'd lost that in some evidence locker somewhere."

Mindy blushes, then shakes her cuff down over it.

"David said I could keep it." She swallows. "He's really helped me out of a hole. Explained the whole thing to Sheriff Cooper on my behalf, that he doesn't think I took anything other than this watch, and that it ought to have been mine to begin with…" She sighs. "That's where I was on the night of the party. When you couldn't find me." Mindy can't quite reach my gaze, but she's still talking, and I'm too eager to hear her role in that terrible night to do anything other than listen. "I knew this watch had to be somewhere, and when David told me about items going missing, I wanted to rescue it. It's an heirloom, you see. Ed's mother gave it to me when we got married. I hadn't taken it when we split up, but the thought of it going missing was just too much to bear. I know I don't have a claim to it, but I also knew Ed wouldn't begrudge me holding onto it." She risks a smile. "I think he must have been watching over me that night, because I knew exactly where to find it, stuffed inside one of the ridiculous little book vaults he kept hidden in the study." She rolls her eyes. "I guess Jessica never had cause to set foot into a room so devoted to learning."

"Don't be mean," I say, gently taking her hand and squeezing. My dislike of Jessica has softened with her passing, and I almost feel sorry for her. *Almost*.

"Anyway, the watch technically belongs to David now, along with the rest of the estate, and he gifted it to me. He also insisted on not pressing charges, so I managed to escape with nothing more than a warning from Sheriff Cooper about my behavior." She grimaces. "A very stern warning."

"I'm glad." I hug her again, grateful that one of my friends, at least, is exactly who I always thought she was.

"As for Louise..." Mindy frowns. "*Simone.* I'm not surprised Ed gave her that name. It had been destined for our daughter, if we'd ever had one." She seems mournful for a moment but soon cheers up. "But I can also understand why she wouldn't want to use it. There are so many secrets people keep, Cassie. I wish we could all learn to be a bit more open about things."

"I don't know about that," I say, bracing as Joe strolls over towards us.

"Ladies." He tips an invisible cap and carries on walking, calling over his shoulder to me as he passes.

"Phone's ringing off the hook in there. Looks like there's going to be plenty for our new lifestyle manager to do once she starts work."

I laugh, but I don't dismiss his words. I'm still not sure how I feel about taking on the role at Serenity Suites after everything that's happened, but I also don't know where else I have to go. David Patterson's plans to redevelop my whole street remain unchanged, and even with the goodwill payout he offered, I don't know if I can face house-hunting, at my age. With a sigh, I look down at my hands, thinking over how close I came to seeing the end of everything, and decide that if I could get through that, I can certainly manage a few ailing seniors. I get to my feet, and Mindy watches me, her expression concerned.

"Where are you going?"

"To find David Patterson. It looks like he now holds the majority interest in Serenity Suites, which means I guess he's my new boss." I smile, deciding to make the best of the curveball life has thrown me. "We are going to have to devise one heck of a PR campaign if we don't want the project to sink before we even open our doors."

Mindy smiles and stands next to me, sliding her arm companionably through mine.

"If there's anyone that can manage that, Cassie Clinton, it's you."

• • • •

The End

About the Author

When Rachel Beattie isn't writing stories, she's usually reading them - especially of the cozy mystery variety. A lifelong devotee of Agatha Christie, she loves putting ze little grey cells to work and is especially fond of anything that can make her laugh while she's collecting a clue or two.

• • • •

Join her mailing list[1] for more information, new release news, exclusives and bonus content.

---

1. https://mailchi.mp/003ddbbcc668/newsletter-subscribers

Also by Rachel Beattie

A Serenity Suites Cozy Mystery
Cassie Clinton and the First Fatality
Double Trouble for Cassie Clinton
Cassie Clinton and the Triple Threat

A Slice of Life Cozy Mystery
Love, Lies and Pumpkin Spice
Wed, Dead and Gingerbread
Crime Scenes and Blackcurrant Cream
Spirits, Spells and Caramel
Broken Hearts and Strawberry Tarts
A Slice of Life Cozy Mystery Books 1-3

A Very Merry Murder Mystery
The Santa Slaughter
The First Date Disaster
The Body in the Bookstore
The Harmony Inn Homicide

The Scandal at the Spa
The Babysitter Bungle
The Campground Killer
The Deadly Dinner Party
The Flower Shop Felony
A Very Merry Murder Mystery Books 1-3